THE EMPTY PLACE

BY OLIVIA A. COLE

Cloud Parliament
Dear Medusa
Time to Roar
The Truth About White Lies
Where the Lockwood Grows

FALOIV

A Conspiracy of Stars
An Anatomy of Beasts

THE TASHA TRILOGY

Panther in the Hive
The Rooster's Garden

THE
EMPTY
PLACE

OLIVIA A. COLE

LITTLE, BROWN AND COMPANY
New York   Boston

Copyright © 2024 by Olivia A. Cole

Bird in tree silhouette and tree branch silhouette © andreashofmann7777/Shutterstock.com. Compass © watermelon_k/Shutterstock.com. Tree branch silhouette © sema srinouljan/Shutterstock.com. Tree silhouette © Matus Madzik/Shutterstock.com.

Cover art copyright © 2024 by Islenia Mil. Cover design by Jenny Kimura. Cover copyright © 2024 by Hachette Book Group, Inc. Interior design by Michelle Gengaro-Kokmen.

Little, Brown and Company
Hachette Book Group
1290 Avenue of the Americas, New York, NY 10104
Visit us at LBYR.com

First Edition: November 2024

Little, Brown and Company is a division of Hachette Book Group, Inc. The Little, Brown name and logo are registered trademarks of Hachette Book Group, Inc.

Little, Brown and Company books may be purchased in bulk for business, educational, or promotional use. For information, please contact your local bookseller or the Hachette Book Group Special Markets Department at special.markets@hbgusa.com.

Library of Congress Cataloging-in-Publication Data
Names: Cole, Olivia A., author.
Title: The empty place / Olivia A. Cole.
Description: First edition. | New York : Little, Brown and Company, 2024. | Audience: Ages 8–12. | Summary: "A girl falls into a parallel universe where all lost things go." —Provided by publisher.
Identifiers: LCCN 2023051681 | ISBN 9780316449427 (hardcover) | ISBN 9780316449533 (ebook)
Subjects: CYAC: Space and time—Fiction. | Missing persons—Fiction. | Lost and found possessions—Fiction. | Friendship—Fiction. | Parent and child—Fiction.
Classification: LCC PZ7.1.C6429 Em 2024 | DDC [Fic]—dc23
LC record available at https://lccn.loc.gov/2023051681

ISBNs: 978-0-316-44942-7 (hardcover), 978-0-316-44953-3 (ebook)

Printed in Indiana, USA

LSC-C

Printing 1, 2024

For Asha

SOMETIMES HENRY WAKES up thinking her father is alive. She stopped dreaming about him three months ago—at least every night—but there are still nights when she wakes up and hears his voice. She tries hard not to believe in ghosts, and for months, that's what it sounded like when she'd open her eyes in the dark and hear him talking. But by now, she knows the truth.

Tonight when she hears his voice, she gets up from her bed, her feet panther-soft across the carpet. She goes to the door, then down the hall. From there she can look over the banister down at the living room, where her mother hunches over a laptop at the dining room table, speakers blaring. She has her back to Henry, Henry's father's face grinning through the screen.

"Now, if you've been watching me for a long time, then you already know what I'm about to say!"

Henry knows this YouTube episode by heart. She can't see it all from here, but she remembers that behind her father is a mountain. He's surrounded by thick green.

"If you ever get lost, go downhill! Well, that's what you're supposed to do. But if you know me, you know I always go up. I go to the highest point because if I'm lost, I want to see the whole world before the vultures get me!"

He laughs, and the camera follows him up a trail. On-screen, his thirty million subscribers still have his thousands of videos to watch. On-screen, it's almost as if he never went missing.

"I've got my compass here just in case," he says. He holds it up to the camera. It's the one Henry and her mother gave him on Father's Day a couple of years ago. Engraved on the back is *Home is the best North Star.*

Henry's mother had that put on especially for him, and this is the part of the video when her mother's shoulders start to shake. Henry hates this part. The part where they both know he's the last person on earth who should have gotten lost and there's nothing they can do. Her father was an experienced hiker, but the rangers said he must have gotten separated from his personal location device. He must have lost his map.

The rangers said the only thing they had to go on was

conjecture. Henry heard *conjecture* so many times that eventually she looked it up: It meant "a conclusion formed with incomplete information," which Henry decided was a fancy way of saying "we have no idea what happened to your dad." Either way, no number of "conjectures" brought Henry's father back, and Quinvandel Forest was big enough that even after months of searching, they never found a trace of him.

Over two thousand people get lost hiking every year, though not all of them on their daughter's eleventh birthday.

Still, Henry's father got lost. He wasn't the first. He wasn't even the last. But he was one.

CHAPTER 1

enry's twelfth birthday party starts in an hour, and she's six blocks away from her house, sifting through a mound of trash.

This empty lot used to be a garden before Mr. Phillips moved away, and like with most empty lots, no one is really sure where the trash in it comes from—no one ever remembers littering. Henry thinks one bottle cap must put out a signal, and trash from all over slowly crawls there to gather. It made her sad to watch the garden fade. But now whenever she's starting a new collage, she comes here first.

"Anything good?" Ibtihaj joins Henry like she said she would. Her house is six blocks in the other direction, and always has been.

"Just trash."

"Henry." Ibtihaj rolls her eyes playfully because Henry says this every time. *Just trash*, when trash is what they're looking for.

Ibtihaj is the only one who calls Henry, Henry. It's one of two things that made them friends to begin with. The first was that in third grade they were both eating cheese pizza on a day that cheese pizza wasn't being served in the lunch line. Henry is a vegetarian and Ibtihaj is Muslim, and they decided that the chili being served that day in the cafeteria was mysterious and probably not halal. Both girls have permission slips signed so whenever there is something they can't eat on the menu, they are given flavorless rectangles of cheese pizza.

The second thing that made them friends was that when Ibtihaj sat down next to Henry, she asked her name. Henry told her—Henrietta—and Ibtihaj studied her the way Henry now knows she studies everyone.

Does anyone call you Henry? Ibtihaj asked.

No, Henry said, *because usually people shorten it to Etta.*

Can I call you Henry? Ibtihaj asked.

Henry decided that yes, she could. And they have been friends ever since.

Together now, they both scan the dirt. They've only ever had one fight, and it was over who got to keep the M-shaped piece of pipe they found here once. Henry let her have it. Henry remembers that fight especially because it was two days before her father disappeared and Ibtihaj brought the pipe the day after as an offering. It's still in Henry's drawer. And her dad is still gone.

Henry holds up a calcified red wire. It's bent into the shape of a perfect cursive *O*.

"Nice," Ibtihaj says. She has something behind her back. "I brought you your present," she says. "Do you want it now or later?"

"Later."

Ibtihaj shrugs and slips it into her back pocket. Then she crouches down to eye the trash more closely.

"Working on something new?"

"Maybe. I'm done with the metal-theme one. I'll show you."

"Yay."

Henry unearths something small and black with the stick she's been using as a shovel. The tire of a Lego car.

"Good find," Ibtihaj says.

Henry nods and put it in the canvas bag that hangs from her shoulder. Ibtihaj notices the bag not only because she notices most things but also because it's not the one Henry usually carries—this one is beige and on the side is printed NATURE IS NEUTRAL in big green letters. Then smaller underneath: KEEP PUBLIC LANDS PUBLIC.

"Was that your dad's?" Ibtihaj asks, but she knows that it had to have been. And because Ibtihaj notices everything, she also notices how Henry does not look her in the eye when she answers.

"Yeah. My old one got a hole in the bottom corner. I'd found a cool copper washer, and it fell out on my walk home."

"Bummer. Was definitely time for a new bag."

"Yeah."

Henry is thinking about her father, and she thinks Ibtihaj is too. She's never said that she misses him—not to Ibtihaj and not even to her mother. People always avoid the big things. She doesn't know why other people do, but she knows why she does. She's afraid the missing will get bigger. And bigger. Sometimes the feeling of missing him is so big it feels like Quinvandel itself. Can you get lost in a feeling?

"I'm okay," Henry says. She scrapes dirt out of the toy tire.

"I can't always tell," Ibtihaj says.

There are other things Henry is avoiding too. Her therapist told her that her mother had mentioned Henry had been quiet. She wonders if Ibtihaj thinks she has too. Henry could ask, but that's another thing she thinks she has to avoid, the same way Henry knows how much her mother cries but never asks her about it. Just like how Henry's mother never asks why Henry is quiet. A careful balance: like maybe they both hope that if they stay very still and silent, the sadness won't swallow them whole.

Henry thinks it's a little late for that.

"Did you invite anybody else to your birthday party?" Ibtihaj asks while they sift through more junk.

"Yeah right."

She laughs, and Henry does, too, to show she's okay.

"Let me guess," Ibtihaj says. "Your mom invited Uncle Cecil."

Now Henry really does laugh. She and Ibtihaj have been friends long enough for her to know how things go in Henry's family. Henry's parents, social butterflies. Henry, their earthworm daughter. They were both happiest when surrounded by people, buzzing around. Hiking. Parks. Horseback riding. Henry? Long, slow walks with Ibtihaj, sometimes not talking for an hour. She once almost missed a piece of volcanic glass out in the woods because she was trying to keep up with her dad, the way he marched through the trees. They were different in that way, and they both knew it. *An outdoor father and an indoor daughter*, her father had said. *One spry and one shy.*

Henry turns to Ibtihaj.

"Can I ask you a question?"

Ibtihaj looks surprised. Also maybe relieved.

"Definitely."

"Do you think I'm shy?"

Ibtihaj gives it some thought. This is another reason she and Henry are best friends. Ibtihaj takes her time.

"No," she says finally. "You don't have a problem talking to people. You don't even mind, like, confronting people. Like last year. Melinda."

Henry nods, remembering. They go to school with Melinda, who is the kind of person who laughs at everything, including people. Including Eun-ji, who was learning English last year. There was a day in art class when Melinda thought Eun-ji's accent was funny, and when she laughed she looked at Henry and expected Henry to laugh too. Henry wasn't sure if it was because they were both white or because they'd gone to school together for a while and Eun-ji was new. It was the sort of thing that made Henry angry, and she had told Melinda to stop it; then she asked Eun-ji if she wanted to switch desks that day. And they did. But this year Eun-ji had switched schools. Henry and Ibtihaj privately blamed Melinda, and neither had spoken to her since.

"Why do you ask?" Ibtihaj says. She unearths a really good tiny spring.

"Just wondering."

"Are you thinking about your dad?" Ibtihaj asks.

Henry hadn't realized she was staring at Quinvandel. The forest was so big and the town so small that there was no escaping it, really. It was always over her shoulder or around the corner. That was part of the reason her father wanted to live here. His own private forest. Adventure always within

arm's reach when the house began to feel too small. Trying
to ignore the forest is like trying to ignore a wolf chewing on
your ankle. It's always right there, and Henry is always looking at it, knowing that somewhere inside it, her father got lost.

"Yeah," Henry answers.

Ibtihaj shifts.

"I haven't said anything, but... did you hear they're doing
a memorial? A one-year thing? The mayor's office."

Henry had not heard of this. It makes her feel cold.

"My mom probably knew. Maybe that's why she asked
Uncle Cecil to stay after the party for a few days."

"Distraction."

"Yeah. She's good when she's busy."

Henry's mother works extra shifts at the hospital most
days. Henry wishes she were old enough to do that too.
Instead, she digs through trash.

"Blueprint?" Ibtihaj says suddenly.

Just one word, but Henry grins.

"Definitely."

A moment later they're crouched in the dirt, dumping out
all the things Henry has collected so far: three letters from a
computer keyboard, a short length of tiny chain. Other little
pieces of nothing that she would turn into something. Ibtihaj
uses a shard of plastic to draw a big rectangle in the dust.

"You first," she says when she's finished.

They take turns adding one piece. A dust collage, they used to call it when they were littler. But as they started spending their allowance money on the good kind of glue and strong canvas, they'd started to think of dust collages differently. They felt like blueprints. Sometimes Ibtihaj will put a piece somewhere Henry didn't expect. It makes Henry change her own mind about what she'll place next. Nothing is stuck, because it's just in the dust—not a real collage, glued down. With dust collages, she can change anything.

They admire their work when they're finished. It's messy and strange: Screws grow from the bottom of the rectangle like robot flowers.

"I hate to mess it up," Ibtihaj says. "This is a really good one."

"Wanna leave it?"

"We could see if raccoons come and add anything overnight."

Henry giggles, imagining the not-quite-human handprints decorating their work.

"Let's leave it and come back tomorrow," she decides. "But not the red wire. It's too good."

Ibtihaj plucks it out of the dust and hands it over.

"Because what if the raccoons took it?" she says, eyes wide. "My dad already says they're too smart. They know how to open our trash cans."

"What would they use the wire for?"

"Inventions!" Ibtihaj cries.

They come up with raccoon inventions the whole walk home—grappling hooks for climbing into dumpsters, tightropes to cross from roof to roof. It feels good to laugh. Henry's still laughing when they get to her block and see Uncle Cecil's car in the driveway. Uncle Cecil is standing at the front door surrounded by a suitcase and two duffel bags. He always packs most of his house every time he comes to visit. Henry calls to him:

"Do you need help carrying anything?"

He wheels on her, looking annoyed. She was a little afraid of Uncle Cecil when she was little, but now she knows that's just the way he looks.

"On your birthday?" he snorts. And that's just the way he sounds. "Not likely. Where's your mom? I knocked but no answer."

"Probably out back setting up."

"Way too much food, I bet," he mutters. "Way too much everything."

"Probably."

Once inside, he finds his own way to the guest room. Henry can hear her mother come in the back door, then go to the kitchen, opening and closing drawers. When Henry walks in, Ibtihaj at her heels, Henry's mother looks up from the tray of crackers she's spreading into a fan pattern.

"Mom, Uncle Cecil is here."

"Oh, good. Can you carry the potato salad out to the back-yard? Tracy and Willow are out there already."

Tracy is Mom's colleague, an ER nurse. Willow is her older, cool daughter, who wears all black and gives Henry Ziploc smiles, tight and contained. Henry wonders why they're here, but she doesn't ask. She always has questions like these, things that never make it out into the world.

Do you think Dad found a cave?

Do you think he went to the top of the mountain, like he always said he would if he got lost?

If so, why didn't they find him up there?

Do you ever wonder how any of this is possible?

She's found that many people don't like her questions, and especially not her mother. So Henry chooses to keep her questions stacked neatly inside and carries the potato salad to the backyard. She and Ibtihaj lurk around by the bushes, watching more guests arrive. Henry wishes she could go upstairs and glue things to canvas.

"Who's that?" Ibtihaj whispers.

She's looking at Mr. Jordan and his partner, Mr. Jeff, who have just walked in the gate.

"They own that antique store my mom is always going to," Henry tells her. "I guess they're friends."

"She invited them to your birthday party?"

13

This makes Henry pause. Tracy. Willow. Mr. Jordan and Mr. Jeff. It dawns on Henry slowly—the realization that this isn't her birthday anymore. This is the day her father disappeared. And it always will be. The raccoon jokes feel very far away.

Her mother comes out carrying a stack of plates. Henry wonders if she thinks that having lots of people at the house will shrink all the big things that they're both avoiding.

"How about you put your bag down?" she says, nodding at the now-mostly-empty sack on Henry's shoulder. Henry wonders if she notices the bag is his.

Henry nods, but she keeps the bag on her shoulder. Keeping it on means it's one less thing to pick up when she sneaks to her room—maybe Mom won't notice. Henry doesn't even like potato salad.

Eleanor arrives. Eleanor is another of Henry's mother's friends from the hospital, a woman with an always-smiling smile and hands that are always moving. It's hard for Henry to like Eleanor. She talks so much. So many questions. And now she's coming right toward Henry.

"Happy birthday, Henrietta! Twelve! So close to being a teenager. How does that feel? Oh, that bag, I love that. *Nature is neutral.* It was your dad's, wasn't it? Of course it was. He was so smart, wasn't he? Such a talker. I remember he got into an argument with my ex-husband when they were trying to

14

keep people from hiking that trail without paying a toll for the Paiute. Your dad hiked the river and went six miles out of his way just to hike that mountain for free. Isn't that just so *him?*"

She laughs. Henry's smile feels like a wire. People like to tell Henry stories about her father like she was a baby when he died—they forget that she is not a baby, and that if they remember, then she remembers. When they tell her he found dinosaur fossils, she knows which ones. A hundred-year-old moonshine hideout—he FaceTimed her mother from it. Paintings and pottery and arrowheads. Henry knows where they are in the basement, lined up on white-lit glass shelves. Her father found caves no one knew existed.

Eleanor moves on to talk to Mr. Jordan. Ibtihaj has been standing next to Henry silently, and now Henry sees that her best friend's face looks full of something. Something that wasn't there before. Henry takes a deep breath. She wants this day to be over.

"My mom hasn't told me happy birthday," Henry says quietly.

And this is another reason Henry loves Ibtihaj, because Ibtihaj doesn't gasp or screech or careen. She's quiet for a little while, taking her time. Then she says simply, "I'm sorry."

"It's okay."

"Are you gonna say something?"

Henry shakes her head just as her mother calls for her. As

Henry walks over, she thinks maybe she'll say it now, but she doesn't. She has a hard time looking at Henry. Unasked question: *Does she blame me?* Henry has wondered more than once if maybe her father wouldn't have gone as far into Quinvandel if his poky daughter had gone with him.

"Help me carry out the rest of the food?" her mother asks.

"Sure."

Inside, the house is quiet. Everyone is outside. It's what people call a perfect summer night—even in the kitchen, Henry can smell the bug torches. She waits by the counter while her mother digs a fruit tray out of the fridge. From here she can see Ibtihaj talking to her dad, Mr. Umar, who has just arrived. And past them, past everyone, is Quinvandel.

The kitchen is quiet for a while. Henry knows it's because her mother is looking too. They do this.

"What are you thinking about?" her mom asks, now passing the fruit tray.

Answer: wondering if we'd both be gone if we'd gone in together. Henry knows her mother doesn't really want to know the answer, though.

"Nothing."

"Okay. You take the fruit. I'll take the veggies."

The yard has gotten busier. The next-door neighbor and her four little kids. Other adults Henry only sort of recognizes. She wishes again that she were in her room and wonders if anyone knows what today is. Have other people kept track of the days like she and her mother have? At least some people know it's her birthday—there are a few wrapped presents set on a table by the food. Henry is so good at being polite, but she wonders if everyone knows this party is a disguise.

"Henrietta, can you take this Sprite to Willow?"

Henry's mom speaks to her only when she's asking her to do something.

Henry takes the Sprite to Willow, Ibtihaj with her just because.

"My mom said to give you this."

Older girls make Henry a little nervous. Willow is tall and cool with hair on her legs, and she acts like nothing is a big deal.

"It's been a year, right?" Willow says, accepting the Sprite. "Is that what the party's for?"

There's a plant that grows at the back of Henry's yard—it sprouts little pods filled with thick white fluff. Henry thinks her throat has transformed into one of those pods. No words can get around it.

"It's her birthday," Ibtihaj says.

"Oh," Willow says, and actually looks surprised. Henry

can see her wheels turning, putting the pieces together. "He got lost on...?"

"On...my birthday."

"That sucks," Willow says. She says it like she really means it. "That sucks a *lot.*"

Henry just nods.

"Do you miss him?" Willow asks, and cracks open the Sprite.

It's a simple question, but to Henry it somehow feels like she grabbed Henry's shoulders and shook.

"Yes."

Ibtihaj touches Henry's shoulder in a way that makes it seem like what Willow said was the wrong thing.

"Was that rude?" Willow says, widening her eyes a little over the top of the can. "Sorry. I'm not always sure."

"It's okay. Nobody has ever actually asked."

Now Willow's eyes narrow back to normal.

"People just kind of assume, don't they?"

"Yeah."

"Sometimes missing people is complicated."

Henry isn't exactly sure what she means by that—part of her feels like she's sinking into a puddle and that she should walk away before it flows over the top of her shoes. Part of her wants to see what it feels like to let it. Henry knows Willow's dad used to live with her, but Henry hasn't seen him in two years. She wants to ask, *Is yours missing too?* She can almost feel the question in her mouth like a cherry pit. Her questions tend to stop just before she spits them out.

Then Henry's mother is calling again, but Henry's not paying attention. It's not until Uncle Cecil shouts that she looks toward the house.

"If you don't blow these candles out, I will!" he says.

The cake is all lit up on the table that Henry's mother spread a white cloth on. There's never a warning when something reminds Henry of her father. This time it's the white cloth—it reminds her of the cloth on the table at the memorial service. There was a fan that made the edge of it ripple by the floor.

As Henry walks to the table, she feels a bit like a robot: one foot in front of the other. And she still feels like a robot as she smiles while the people her mother invited sing "Happy Birthday." Over the past year, Henry has gotten some practice in allowing her mind to float away, and she does it now too. She keeps floating as the tiny sparks of her twelve candles sway. She keeps floating even when her mother, beside her at the table, stands up very slowly.

Even when Ibtihaj's hand grips Henry's shoulder.

Even when Henry hears Willow whisper, "No way. No way. No way."

No one is looking at Henry or the cake. They're staring

past her, at Quinvandel, which, at the end of the day, has finally turned into a black smudge. There are only traces of daylight left. It's enough light for Henry to see that everyone wears the same face, all their mouths open.

When her mother starts screaming, Henry finally comes down from the place she slipped away to.

There's just enough light to see a shadow that has broken away from the forest, separate from the smudge of it. The shadow moves slowly up the yard, toward where everyone stands staring. It's tall and slender and pale. There's just enough light to see that the shadow is not a shadow, but a person.

There's just enough light to see that the shape limping toward them is Henry's dad.

CHAPTER 2

The windows on the hospital's fifth floor look out over the top of Quinvandel, endless miles of trees like a carpet rolled out to the sun. Looking at it, Henry can almost smell the cedar and pine. The sweet, dark smell of decomposing leaves. Her father thought she didn't like the outdoors, but that was never exactly true. Henry just loves it in a different way.

But cedar and pine are just a trick of memory—the real smells around her are more sour: The burny-ness of disinfectant covers everything else up. Instead of the songs of birds and the rustle of chipmunks, all Henry hears is the beep and sigh of the machine that's helping her father heal.

"Do you want to go grab us something from the vending machine?" her mother asks.

After so much silence, the sudden sound of her voice makes Henry jump where she sits by the window. She turns slowly to look.

Her mother has her chair pulled up close to the hospital bed, her hand latched around Henry's father's. She hasn't taken her eyes off him since he came walking out of the forest the day before. The circles under her eyes look like they were carved. Even now, she barely looks at Henry. And Henry barely looks at him. When she does, she feels a little like her head is spinning.

"Okay."

Henry's mother nods at her purse, and once Henry fishes around for some bills and coins, she slips out into the hallway. It's quiet out here. But at least not as quiet as the room where her parents are.

Henry stares at the rows of Doritos and Snickers bars in the vending machine. She's supposed to be getting something for her mother, of course, because her father is sedated. That meant, she learned, that they gave him medicine to make him sleep. She thinks part of why her head keeps spinning is because when he came out of Quinvandel, he looked like her father and was even dressed like her father, but he was saying things that didn't make sense.

I found the land of Truth.

I have discovered a land where the children roam with deer!

He had looked right at her, but she wasn't sure he could actually see her. Or her mother. Now Henry looks through the vending machine at the Payday candy bar, because that's what her father would want. But will he remember that when he wakes up? Maybe his body has returned, but he left his mind in Quinvandel? In some ways, his mind was in Quinvandel before he disappeared too. Or if not there, everywhere else. Sometimes Henry looked at the map on his wall in the basement and all its colorful pins—red for *been there*, yellow for *next*, blue for *one day*—and she imagined his brain the same way. She wonders, *If I were a pin on a map in his head, what color would I be?*

With her mind somewhere else, half the coins slip out of Henry's hands, clinking to the floor and rolling underneath the vending machine.

"Crap."

She crouches down to look, but they've rolled to the back, so she scoots around the corner of the machine, reaching under into the sticky dust.

"It's more than miraculous," someone is saying, walking from the direction blocked by the vending machine. They stop in front of it. "It's *impossible*. A year? He's mostly clean. Fairly nourished. It doesn't make sense."

"Miracles don't usually make sense," someone else replies. "He was so many people's hero before. Imagine what people will say when the word gets out! It's incredible."

One of them puts change into the machine. Henry presses herself against it to listen, frozen. The machine thrums against the back of her head as it retrieves their snack.

"You have to wonder how it's possible," the first person says. "The police are waiting until he's more stable, but I was told they're treating it as a possible abduction."

"Abduction? Oh my word..."

"You know how those YouTube people can be. They'll be saying it was aliens."

"Could've been political. Remember when he was on the news for crossing into protected territory? Some people were mad about *keep public land public*. You know that man didn't care about rules."

"Remember when he found that pottery piece? What was it?"

"A sacred urn, maybe?"

"Lord, they had to make him give it back. He had the guts to say *finders keepers* on live television." They chuckle lightly. "Maybe not too far off that someone kidnapped the man."

"Could be. Could be. Either way, thank goodness he's back. If nothing else, for that child's sake."

They wander off down the hall, and Henry listens until

they're out of earshot but doesn't move for what feels like a long time. Henry knows her father would have loved overhearing that conversation. It was one of his favorite parts about what he did—that people would stop him on the street and tell him their kids showed them his channel, that the whole family subscribed to his posts. Millions of people all over the globe, watching Henry's father discover the world. Her mother never minded—she would stand there beaming. But Henry always felt a little like a chalk drawing on concrete. There one minute, gone the next.

Henry can find only a few of the quarters under the vending machine. She gets her mother a bag of Cheez-Its and herself a Payday. Back in the quiet room where her father lies sleeping, Henry eats it peanut by peanut. Her mother has cut some yellow flowers and put them in a vase on the table. Henry recognizes them—lesser celandine. Technically an invasive species, which is the only reason she cut them. She would always get annoyed when Henry's father brought her flowers—*The bees need them more!*

"Remember the Grand Canyon?" she whispers to Henry. It's the first time they've really looked at each other. She's smiling a little. "When the three of us wore matching shirts?"

Henry nods. That was when he first started his channel. It was a very hot day, and Henry remembers the shade the most—the three of them resting and drinking water. She

25

enjoyed that part. When they were all still. When he wasn't looking ahead and around, but at Henry and her mother.

"That was such a fun day," her mother says quietly. She's looking at him again.

"Yeah."

"I can't believe he's here."

"Yeah."

Henry thinks of what the people in the hall said. She wonders if someone would actually kidnap him, or if he was in the trees this whole long year. She wonders about UFOs. Would they have taken him to a world where children run with alien deer? Outside, fog collects over the tops of the forest in the distance. Right now, even though her father is somehow back in the same room with her, the trees feel closer than he does.

"You haven't said much," Henry's mother says.

Her eyes stay on him when she says it. But suddenly Henry is sweating. She feels how she felt when Willow asked if Henry missed him. Not just shaken.

Seen.

Questions Henry will never ask bubble up in her head.

Does she think I didn't miss him?

Does she think I'm not happy that he's back?

What if she thinks I wish he stayed gone?

What if she's right?

CHAPTER 3

enry wakes to the sound of someone whispering her name. The room is shadowy and cold, and she was dreaming about Quinvandel—for a moment she thinks that's where she is. But her cramped arms and legs remind her: She's in the armchair by the window in her father's hospital room, everything dark except for the moon outside and the tower of blinking lights by his bed. Her eyes adjust, and she can make out the slumped form of her mother, sleeping with his hand as a pillow. It's not her mother saying Henry's name.

It's him.

"Henrietta," her father repeats. "Wake up."

Henry snaps up, her hands and feet tingling now that

blood flows into them again. But that's not the only reason. Her whole head feels prickly, too, goose bumps on her arms, because her father's voice sounds cracked and squeaky, like the door to a haunted house.

"Dad?"

"Come here," he murmurs. "Come here, Henrietta."

Henry swallows. The weird glow from the moon and the hospital machines makes her want to stay in the chair. But guilt wraps around her and squeezes like a boa constrictor. This is her father, and he has returned.

"I came all this way to give you something," he says, still in that raspy whisper.

Henry creeps across the slick hospital floor toward his bed. She'd taken her shoes off before curling up in the chair, so her steps are silent. The machines go on beeping rhythmically.

"What?" she whispers. She's afraid her mother will wake up, that she'll panic and call the nurses, or worse, maybe, that she'll start talking to him and crying and Henry will be a chalk drawing again, wiped away. Right now Henry's father is not looking at her—his eyes are still closed—but he's talking. To Henry.

"In my bag," he says. "It's here, isn't it? In my bag."

When he came out of the forest, Henry didn't notice the bag. It's as much a part of him as the green hiking boots he always wore on his adventures. As his audience grew, fancy shoe brands would send him hiking boots to wear for free in exchange for mentioning their names, and he did it. But on his real trips, he would always wear the same pair. Those boots, and the bag he wore at his waist. A fanny pack, Henry's mother called it, teasing, but her father said it was his Superman belt. He was wearing it when he went into the forest on Henry's eleventh birthday. And he was wearing it when he came out on her twelfth.

Now it's in the bin of personal items that the nurses brought after getting him into a sage-green hospital gown. His boots are there, his pants and shirt and jacket. Even his wallet. An entire year and he still has his wallet, which makes Henry think of aliens again, and her skin crawls less. Aliens would have kept his wallet, she thinks. But there's the Superman belt: a buckled waistband attached to a small pack, big enough for things like bandages and a tracker, a pocketknife. A little yellow notebook with a bowling-alley pencil tucked inside that he used to write little notes to himself. Henry rests her hand on the pack now, looking back at him through the gloom of the hospital room.

"Open it," he croaks.

Her fingers shake a little. She had imagined her father showing up alive a million times. More than a million. For every leaf in the forest of Quinvandel, she had imagined a different scenario of her father showing up alive. In some scenarios she'd be at school and would be called to the office and he'd be there waiting, smiling, like a surprise. In another, Henry and her mother would be hiking and they would hear someone calling for help, then find him wandering through the ferns. In others, Henry would be visiting a friend in the hospital and there would be a room with a patient with amnesia whom nobody knew. And even though it didn't make sense, because everyone knows Henry's dad, she'd peek through the door and he'd be there, and suddenly his vision would clear and all his memories would come flooding back.

The truth is somewhere in between. He wandered out of the forest without Henry and her mother going in, and at first he didn't seem to remember. But now it's dark and he's awake and he's saying her name, even if it sounds unsteady. Her mother going on sleeping.

"Open it," he repeats, and this time Henry does, unzipping it slowly and carefully. "I brought it back. For you."

Once the bag is open, Henry is afraid to reach inside. It's so dark in this room, and so is the mouth of the bag. But she takes a deep breath, and in goes her hand. She thinks it's empty at first. And it mostly is. No bear spray, no compass. (No compass. That makes her heart sink.)

The pack is empty except for a square of papers, folded thick.

"Take it out," he whispers. "Over into the light."

Henry pulls the thick square out, then take two steps back toward the window, where moonlight streams in.

A map.

"Inside," Dad croaks.

In the dim light Henry can make out the word *Quinvandel*—the map he was using when he got lost. She unfolds it square by square—she can feel there's something inside, layered under the folds. It falls out into her hand. It's a smooth something, smooth like glass, then the thin line of what feels like string. It's a necklace. She holds it out in the moonlight.

Henry has never liked jewelry—she doesn't even have her ears pierced. But she doesn't think anyone could hold this and not at least stop and stare.

The chain is delicate silver, light and soft like yarn. It ripples over her fingers like water. And then there's the pendant. Round and fat and silver white, catching the moonlight like the surface of a still pond. It's thick enough to be a locket, but there are no hinges. It's like holding that still pond right in her palm.

"It's beautiful," Henry murmurs.

"It's for you. I came all this way to give it to you."

Henry's head is spinning again—she feels a little like crying and a little like throwing up. She's spent the past year being walked through all the steps of grief—the therapist, Ms. June, and all her books and whiteboard illustrations of what she called "sad cycles." But no matter what the advice, it was always the same thing wearing different disguises: moving on, letting go. After a while Henry cried less and stared at the forest more. But now that her father is back, everything Henry let go of comes zooming back. She still hasn't touched him. Something inside her worries that, somehow, he isn't actually real.

"Where have you been?" Henry whispers. The words almost catch in her throat with all her other questions, but this one she sighs out.

"I was lost," he whispers. "But I found the way. I knew I had to come back...and give you...give you what I discovered. My greatest discovery is my gift to you. Happy...happy birthday, Henrietta."

His eyes finally open, but the expression in them is still far away. Henry gets the feeling he's looking at her through a thick fog. But he does see her, and he sees the necklace in her hands, and he goes on staring, eyes shiny with tears. It's not until Henry slowly raises the necklace and drapes it over her head, settling it on her chest, that he finally closes his eyes again. And Henry would never admit it out loud, but she breathes the quietest sigh of relief.

CHAPTER 4

btihaj and her parents dropped off a bean pie while Henry and her mother were at the hospital, and now Henry sits at the counter at home, eating it with a fork straight out of the plate. Henry was supposed to call Ibtihaj, but she still feels dizzy. And then there's the matter of the necklace. Explaining the necklace to her best friend wouldn't be as complicated as explaining how she *feels* about it.

Henry brought home her father's small pack, and her mother didn't question it. With the necklace hidden under Henry's shirt, the pack is now empty except for the map of Quinvandel, and she keeps it close while she sits eating the pie. She had hoped to be alone for a while, but Mom insisted

Uncle Cecil stay to keep watch over Henry while her mother stayed in the hospital with her father. Henry thinks it's a little like being babysat by a grumpy goat.

If she leans sideways, she can see him outside talking on his clunky Bluetooth headphones, his hands making circles while he talks. He visited for Christmas after Henry's father disappeared, and once Henry went to bed, he and her mother had a fight, the sounds of their words stabbing up through her bedroom floor. When Henry asked her mother about it later, she said, *Cecil's my brother. We'll always have our squabbles.*

Henry knew it was more than this. She could tell it was something serious by the way her mother's mouth stayed small the next day. Before Henry's father got lost, when her mother would try to get them all to go visit Uncle Cecil in Lexington, her father would refuse and say, *He's never liked me. Why would I want to visit the man?* It made Henry want to not like Uncle Cecil either. Just to have something in common.

Henry takes another bite of bean pie. It's thick and creamy and good, like custard. The very first time she spent the night at Ibtihaj's house, her father was making one, and the girls helped him do everything from rolling out the dough to mashing the beans. Henry was surprised that it was made with actual beans, even if the name was very clear. *You're always so skeptical*, Ibtihaj said. *Just wait.* Her family moved to Ripling from Philadelphia the same year she and Henry met eating cheese pizza. In Philadelphia, Ibtihaj and her parents would eat bean pie together every week at the mosque after Jumu'ah, the Friday prayer. But after they moved to Ripling, Mr. Umar said, he had to learn to make bean pies himself because no one sold them.

Henry knows how much work goes into making one and appreciates every bite. She imagines Ibtihaj and Mr. Umar and Mrs. Maryam and Ibtihaj's little brother, Boz, together in their big, warm kitchen, each adding cinnamon and nutmeg. They sent this pie knowing that even though Henry's father's reappearing was good news, this was also a hard time.

Next to the pie plate is an iPad, and it makes a tiny *bleep* sound. It's a message from Ibtihaj—a screenshot.

> **IS:** Wow look at this. I guess word is
> getting around.

Henry taps the screenshot so it fills the whole screen. It's the comments section from the very last video her father uploaded. Two days before he went missing. But all the comments are from today and yesterday, as recent as three minutes ago.

> **Yellowstonebro:** I knew you'd come back
> to us!

NotAllWhoWanderAreLost: We've been
waiting! We never gave up hope!

Brb_exploring: When's the next video?
We want to hear everything!

And dozens more screenshots. Hundreds. Henry's stomach clenches around the pie inside it. When *is* the next video? she wonders. How soon would everything go back to normal? Her father off on his adventures, then returning to disappear into the basement to arrange footage. Henry thinks about the collages she has finished since he's been gone. Would he want to see them? All made from trash she's gathered on her long, slow walks.

Henry looks up from the iPad as the door to the back deck slides open bumpily and Uncle Cecil shoulders his way back inside.

"No one calls me when I'm at home," he complains. "But as soon as I leave town, suddenly I'm Mr. Popular."

Henry keeps eating the bean pie. She hoped that eating it straight out of the dish would discourage her being asked to share it. It's not that Henry is even so hungry, but taking the fork from plate to mouth over and over feels nice, almost like a rhythm. But Uncle Cecil doesn't look at her—he stands studying the room, as if he's deciding how things are different since the last time he was here. This time there's no Christmas tree, but there is a father.

"You aren't going to open your gifts?" he says, nodding to the small pile of wrapped presents in the corner. They're mostly from Henry's mother, plus a few things that people she invited to the party brought. The tiny one from Ibtihaj.

Henry hasn't opened any of them. The only gift she cares about is the one hanging around her neck, the pendant hidden by her shirt. The one her father says he came back just to give her. The thing he somehow held on to even when his compass was gone.

"No," is all she says.

Henry didn't tell her mother that he had woken up, that he'd spoken to her. She didn't tell her about the necklace either. After her father had gone back to sleep, Henry sat there in the chair by the window for hours, watching him, wondering if he'd stir again, but he never did. And when the moonlight was replaced with sunlight, flashing in her mother's eyes and waking her up, her face looked so full of hope and sadness that Henry couldn't bear to tell her. She's already missed him for a year—missing even more while she slept seemed unfair, especially because Henry didn't wake her. Henry has decided that if her mother sees the necklace, she'll just tell her she found it in his pack. It's true.

"How are you feeling about all this?" Uncle Cecil says. He

looks like he's considering coming closer. Maybe it's because Henry is leaned over the bean pie like a lynx over a kill, but he chooses to flop down in an armchair instead.

"About all what?" she asks. She suddenly feels a little mad at him, for whatever he said to her mother last Christmas. For whatever reason he supposedly never liked her father. Henry wants to hear him say it: that her father is back. She wants him to admit that maybe he never cared that he was gone to begin with.

"How are you feeling about the fact that your father is alive?" Uncle Cecil says, and at that Henry stops chewing. She didn't think he'd actually say it. And she didn't think he'd actually say *alive*. Everyone else—including Henry, including her mother—has said her father is "back." "Reappeared." "Returned." It's almost as if everyone (except his subscribers) is too polite to admit that for a year, they've considered him dead. For some reason it makes Henry even madder at Uncle Cecil, like he's telling her that they've all been pretending. She doesn't know what to say, so she says nothing.

Uncle Cecil sighs deeply and rubs his short black beard. In some ways Henry looks more like him than she looks like her mother. Her mother's hair is lighter, and Henry's is black, like Uncle Cecil's. They have the same squinty blue eyes, where her mother looks like Bambi. Her mother always says, *Genes are weird*. But right now Henry doesn't want to have anything in common with Uncle Cecil.

"Your dad has always been a survivor," he says. "He was going to keep going until he found all the pieces of himself. And I guess he wasn't done."

Henry puts her fork down. Her brain is starting to get the message that she's had too much pie.

"What do you mean?" she asks. "The pieces of himself?"

"Oh, you know," he says. "It's what people do. They either surround themselves with memories like a pack rat, or they roam looking for something more. That's your dad—all the wandering. Joseph could never hold still. Always on the move. Searching for himself. Has to be *out there*, has to be hunting for the next big thing. Finding the next shiny something."

"Isn't that a good thing?" She thinks of her father's millions of subscribers, all the people in the screenshot Ibtihaj sent who saw his return as the return to adventure. Her father had a sticker on his laptop that said *Adventure is out there*. He sometimes asked her to join him. But mostly he preferred to go alone.

"Sure, it's a good thing," Uncle Cecil says. He's searching inside the folds of the armchair for the remote. "It's a great thing. But when you're a father, some things need to take a back seat. Otherwise you'll be so focused on being the first to discover...I don't know, a new cave or something or other, that you miss what's happening at home."

"You don't even have kids," Henry says, and she knows it comes out more sharply than her mother would consider polite, and being impolite isn't something Henry usually is. But Henry's father was thought to have gone missing in a cave. Hearing Uncle Cecil say the word *cave* feels a little like a spark from a fire popping onto the back of her hand.

He looks up quickly and stares at her for what feels like a long time.

"No," he says. "But I am a son."

He finds the remote and clicks on the TV. They don't have cable—internet was all her father needed. So the few channels the TV has to offer are news.

"Local celebrity Joseph Lightfoot has been found in what doctors are calling a miraculous reappearance," the man on-screen says. "Lightfoot went missing somewhere in the thousands of acres of Quinvandel Forest last year while exploring a cave for his megapopular YouTube channel, *Discovery Joe*. Lightfoot was well known as a vocal opponent of Land Back, which would transfer federal parks to Indigenous stewardship. After his disappearance, recovery efforts were in vain, and after months of searching, he was presumed dead... until Friday, when he was found emerging from the woods, entirely unharmed. Doctors are..."

Uncle Cecil switches the channel. Henry is grateful. At first she had been glad to see her father's face on TV, because it meant it was real. He was back. Alive. But after a while they all kept saying the same things, things everyone knew at this point. What about what she *didn't* know? Where has he been? And how? And why, after so long, has he come back?

"Why did you and my mom fight last Christmas?" The question darts out of Henry's mouth, and she immediately feels a little sick. The thing about asking a question is that you might get an answer. But even though she's mad at Uncle Cecil, Henry feels like she can ask him. He's never been the type to do the thing that so many adults do: say the gentle thing, where they try to make a roof with their words because they think a child can't handle the rain.

He goes on staring at the TV for a minute, so long Henry doesn't think he heard. But then he turns the volume down. He shifts in his seat so he's looking at her.

"Why do *you* think we argued, Henrietta?" he asks.

"Henry," she says. "I go by Henry."

Which isn't exactly true—Ibtihaj is the only one who calls her Henry, but it's when she feels most herself. And maybe also she's avoiding answering his question.

"Why do you think we argued, Henry?" Uncle Cecil fires back.

"Because . . . you didn't like my dad."

41

"No, I didn't," he says flatly, and Henry blinks, shocked. "But I was still very sad. For my sister. And you."

But he hasn't answered the question. And Henry can't make herself ask again. Even if she feels hungry for another reason to be mad at him. To be mad at anyone, maybe.

Uncle Cecil studies her face, then sighs and rubs the bridge of his nose.

"I asked your mother something. I asked…how she knew Joseph didn't just…take off on an adventure," he says hesitantly. "I asked how she knew he was actually missing and that he didn't just…"

He sighs again and stops talking. But Henry finishes for him:

"That he didn't just leave."

Uncle Cecil lets his hand flop down from his face to his knee. Henry wonders if he knows that what he asked her mother, Henry has asked herself a thousand times. It's bad enough to think something terrible. But to hear that someone else thought it, too, makes it seem possible.

"Your dad is famous for a reason, Henry," he finally says. "He's a lovable guy. Did I agree with his stance on public lands? No. Should he have hiked Paiute land deliberately without permission? I don't think so. But your dad would never deliberately leave you."

It made Henry cower a little when people talked about

42

what her dad did on the Paiute land. She had watched You-Tube videos about it after: how it was land under the protection of the Paiute Tribe, and if someone wanted to hike there, they needed permission. Henry's father, she learned, didn't have permission, and that was confusing because he always told her to obey NO TRESPASSING signs and this seemed even worse than walking past one. He said later he did it so more people would watch his videos—they liked to see him doing what he believed in, even if it broke the rules. Henry didn't think that was a very good reason.

But now she is looking at Uncle Cecil, because his voice has changed. He's doing the thing, Henry thinks. Making a roof with his words. He's realizing he rained on her. But rain is supposed to put out fire. Instead Henry feels hot and burny, like if she picked up the fork to eat more pie, the fork would burst into flames.

To distract herself, she stares at the wall ahead of her, at one of her collages that her mother had framed. Henry used more than a hundred pull tabs from soda cans to form a city, then the almost-transparent labels from Pepsi two-liter bottles above it all in a plastic-paper sky. It had hung there for three days before her father noticed.

When Henry doesn't speak, Uncle Cecil turns back to *Wheel of Fortune* and lets the volume fill the room again. While the family on-screen guesses vowels, Henry thinks about what the nurses by the vending machine said. Theories of where her father had gone. Abduction. Aliens. But aliens wouldn't have given her dad a necklace to give to her on her birthday.

After a while, Uncle Cecil's eyes flutter closed. Henry's land across the room, on the bag of things she gathered from the empty lot with Ibtihaj. Lego tires, tiny springs, delicate screws, plastic pieces broken into strange shapes.

Nature is neutral. Her father's bag. And she'd filled it with trash.

It's not because of the pie that Henry feels like throwing up. There's a question that feels like a lump in Henry's throat. And what Uncle Cecil said makes the question grow and grow, too large to swallow. There it is, bigger and bigger:

What if he leaves again?

Her father and his compass and his endless adventures. A daughter who doesn't like mosquitoes, who prefers her cluttered desk, dotted with dried hot glue. And now, his millions of subscribers. *I knew you'd come back to us,* they typed. "Us." Like they were part of his family. Family that *would* tag along with him into the green everything when his own daughter would not.

On the chalkboard of Henry's mind, an equation appears. It suddenly makes perfect sense why he might have left.

Dad is a butterfly—happiest when outside, fluttering from

place to place. But Henry thinks she definitely must be an earthworm. Slow, quiet. A butterfly would always keep moving, wouldn't it?

She goes to the bag of trash and then crosses back to the kitchen, where she tips it into the garbage. Her heart squeezes a little at the sound of the Lego tire clattering down into the dark. She stands there for a moment, considering reaching in for it. But then her eye falls on her father's small pack on the kitchen table, laid next to the pie plate. Inside is the map of Quinvandel, the one that the necklace had been wrapped in.

It feels like a sign.

Henry moves away from the trash can and toward the pack. It's bright green, like a traffic light. Henry thinks of what the therapist said: *Your mother says you've been quiet lately*. Henry's long walks, searching for little pieces to glue together. Looking at the go-green pack, she thinks she might have been searching for the wrong thing.

Henry slips quietly out the back door while Uncle Cecil sleeps. She pauses only to buckle her father's small pack at her waist, Quinvandel waiting there at the back of the yard like a deep green wall. It doesn't look welcoming, but she doesn't think it looks forbidding either. The sun is high, and there are trees and trees and trees. Among them is the narrow path that she always considered her father's.

After the search parties, Henry never went into the forest

again. Her mother never needed to tell her not to—Henry was not that kind of kid. *Indoor girl*, she thinks as she moves toward the path. *Today will be different*, she decides. Today she has a map with her father's handwriting on it. Today she will walk where he walked, and Henry can almost picture his smile in her head when she tells him everything she'll have seen.

When Henry reaches the mouth of her father's path, she's clutching the map in one hand and resting the other over the pendant. The smell of the forest is strong and familiar—cedar and pine, dead leaves. She hears her father's whisper: *I found the way back to give you what I discovered.*

Henry tells herself that by the time he wakes up again, she will be new. The kind of daughter that goes with him. The kind that he can see.

Maybe the kind that makes him want to stay.

CHAPTER 5

Noon inside the forest is different than noon out in the open. The leaves are like a green dome overhead. When Henry's father first disappeared, the neighbors and the police talked about doing more and more search parties, but Jemmy, her father's cameraman, said there was no point. Not if they were going to search the forest. If Joseph Lightfoot was lost in the caves, they would need experts for that. Around this time, Henry checked out a book from the library about bloodhounds and learned they have three hundred million scent receptors in their noses. They brought a bloodhound from two counties over to search for Henry's father, and for a little while she was sure about the bloodhound. But the dog never found anything.

Still, Henry and her mother walked up and down this path a lot in those first weeks. Surrounded by neighbors who meant well, who carried hope. Henry remembers slapping at mosquitoes, always looking over her shoulder to make sure she could still see the house. Even when she went around only one curve of the path, she would feel shaky and sweaty, like the forest that had swallowed her father whole might still be hungry. She feels a little like that now too. But the forest spit him out. He walked this path. Henry sees what looks like a footprint, dried in mud, and she pauses to place her foot in it. She wonders why she doesn't recognize the tread of his favorite boots, the boots he wore everywhere.

"I'm going to learn everything." The words sound loud in this big, quiet place.

She keeps moving.

Henry can still see her house when she looks back. But she can almost see why her father loves it out here, where it feels like the wild. The leaves and the insects all sing their own songs. She doesn't plan to go far, because she hasn't brought water, only her father's little pack. But the path is well worn and clearly marked, and she tries to imagine walking in silence with her father, ignoring the mosquitoes. *Or maybe it wouldn't be silence*, she thinks. Maybe out here she would find something to say.

As Henry rounds a bend, she pauses to take the map out of

the pack. The lines that make up Quinvandel spread across it like veins, and here and there are her father's notes. Tiny black etches in pen, as hard to read as ever. But she can make out little things like *possible sinkhole* or *animal den*. Nearby she sees deer tracks set in mud, but no prints from hiking boots. She imagines all the things that a tracker knows to look for that are tinier and more hidden than a footprint. Broken twigs, crushed leaves, a branch disturbed. When she and her mother came up this path with the search parties, they weren't looking for any of that. They were just hoping for a miracle. *And we got one*, she thinks. One year later.

Now Henry reaches for the necklace under her shirt. It fits perfectly in her palm. Wherever he was, she thinks this necklace means he didn't forget about them, about her. He made his way back to give her this. And Henry knows that should be good enough. Her father is back. But she can't push all the questions out: What is out here in the woods, in the world, that calls so loudly to her father, and once he wakes up, will it keep calling? *Adventure is out there.*

Now the head-spinning feeling is back—like Henry is on a Ferris wheel that's going too fast. She thinks of the screen name of one of the commenters on her father's very last video—NotAllWhoWanderAreLost. And that's the biggest question of all, she thinks: If her father wasn't lost... where was he? And why did he stay so long?

She looks down at the map in her left hand. She flips it over, checking the blank back side for any other notes. Nothing. And the front side she can barely read.

And then it hits her. *The map isn't special; it was just paper he wrapped the necklace in*, she realizes. *It's not a sign, and Dad never would have thought I'd come out here. He thinks I'm an indoor girl.*

Her cheeks flush with embarrassment. She slowly folds the map and returns it to her father's pack, then turns on the path. This isn't where she belongs, and this isn't where he wanted her. She takes the first step back toward home.

Her foot finds nothing but empty space.

The spinning Ferris wheel in Henry's head seems to creak and jerk for the long moment before she falls.

Down through emptiness. Crumbling soil falling with her into the dark. The air is suddenly cold and rushing. It happens too fast for her to think anything beyond one word: *sinkhole*. The ground around here, her father told her once, is made of limestone, and it thins out, drops away. The ground can open up like a yawn and plunge straight down into hidden caves.

Henry might be screaming. The cold air fills her up, and then she hits what must be water. She sinks fast, so fast she can't begin to swim. Faster than a stone, as if a current spirals her down to the sediment at the bottom of that underground river, where the white cave fish swim in the dark. And then she's sinking through that, too, the layers of sand and grit rough and quick past her cheeks. Slimy cave plants slicking through her hair. Her fingers claw through it all, but nothing holds.

Whatever is under the grit, Henry falls through that too. And that's when she realizes something is wrong, something is not normal, because she can't still be falling and this still be a fall. This can't be a sinkhole and also a cave and also a river and also quicksand, which she is now sinking down through also. Fast and gritty, billowing around her in sandy bubbles, everything black. She can't still be falling, because this isn't just falling. And all the while the Ferris wheel in her head is spinning and spinning, and it's not until the first full thought forms in her brain—*Where will I be when I stop falling?*—that Henry finally finds her way to ground.

Except now she's not falling down, but *up*, like a geyser is under her back. The earth isn't yawning anymore, but sneezing, and it sneezes Henry out, covered in black-and-green snot. Up and then down, landing hard on her back, eyes squeezed shut.

And when she opens them, she's looking up into the face of a creature with fangs that glow like stars.

CHAPTER 6

Everything around Henry is green. So deep and green that the white of the creature's teeth leaves a spot behind her eyes when she blinks. The creature's eyes are white, too, and as flat as snow on the surface of a frozen lake. A furry but snaky body. Tufts of white feathers around its neck and down the backs of its four thick legs. Henry almost expects the air to be cold—the animal looks like it belongs on the tundra. But they're surrounded by forest and hot August air. She doesn't know how she could have fallen so far and still ended up aboveground. She doesn't have time to think about how.

The creature snorts a blast of air from its mouth, first cold and then hot. It makes her shudder. At this small movement, the animal seems to blink—a filmy eyelid sliding sideways across the icy eyeball. And then there are those teeth again. Dripping icicles. Clear and shiny, sharp and wet. Not from melting, but with saliva.

Henry begins to slowly crawl backward. She's been told that with bears you're supposed to make a lot of noise as you hike. Give the bears plenty of time to hear you and move off. But if you actually see one, you're supposed to stay calm, move slowly, wave your arms slowly. *Identify yourself as human*, her father always said. He had run into bears at least ten times. Lynx. Mountain lions. Never a scratch. But Henry thinks that this animal, whatever it is, is way too close, and if it's anything like a bear, being close—this close, so close—might make it want to attack.

Henry keeps inching backward and tries not to breathe. Ten feet away from the creature. Fifteen feet. It doesn't seem to be looking at her anymore, its long-fanged snout aimed somewhere off to the right. Henry has been told you should never run from a bear, because it'll always catch you. But this isn't a bear. She doesn't know what it is. In spite of her screaming heart, Henry can't help but think: *I discovered something.* Next to her fear, excitement swells like a hot-air balloon. If she could just get home and tell her father . . .

But then she slips, and under her shirt the pendant slides sideways, the delicate chain making a sudden clinking sound. Now the white creature with fangs like stalactites jerks its wolflike, bearlike, lizardlike face back in her direction. It takes one step, then two, and its body moves in a liquid way, like a snake through water. Wolf-bear-lizard-snake. Henry's breath catches in her throat like it's turned solid.

And then she runs. She knows she's not supposed to. But this isn't a bear, and her desire to discover something is smaller than her desire to survive. All she can think and feel is *get away get away get away.*

Henry streaks through the trees, slapped by branches and caught by thorns. She doesn't look back and doesn't need to—she can feel the crash and rumble of the creature through the earth. It seems to shake the whole forest. But she keeps going, zigzagging, running around trunks so big they must be redwoods, though she knows redwoods don't grow in this part of the country. She leaps over a cluster of ferns so thick they look prehistoric. *I am definitely off the path*, she thinks, and this panics her more. She's never been off the path.

The creature roars, a strange searing sound that makes her stumble. Ahead there's a break in the trees, and her heart leaps. It can't be her backyard—the angle is wrong. But perhaps *someone*'s backyard. Someone with bear spray or even a hunting rifle that they can fire into the sky. She stumbles again and swears she feels the tip of an ice-cold tongue on her elbow.

Then Henry bursts out of the tree cover and into the blinding noon sun. It leaves her unable to see anything at all, but she keeps running anyway, hoping that by the time her vision clears she'll be on someone's back porch.

Instead, Henry slams straight into a person, and the force and speed sends them both flying to the ground, where they land in a wheezing pile. She's already clambering up, afraid the creature is there with them.

"The thing—the bear thing—" she stammers.

The glare of the sun mellows. Henry looks around, and the creature is gone.

She can see the tree line of the forest plainly now. But there's no luminous wolf-snake-bear pacing its edge with icicle fangs bared. The forest is serene. She can hear birdsong, tunes she doesn't recognize.

Now a shout, not her own. It's the person Henry ran into, and they're trying to get her attention, but she can't understand the words. She turns to them quickly, ready to apologize and explain. But her hands and legs are shaking. Maybe this is adrenaline—Dad talked about this the first time he came home after a brush with a mountain lion and her cubs. How his body was able to be strong and smart in the moment, but afterward all his muscles transformed into tubes of jelly. It feels like even Henry's brain is jelly, and instead of apologizing or explaining, her mouth makes a squeaking sound. Then she collapses back onto the ground.

The stranger stands over her, hands on hips, studying her.

The stranger is a boy. He wears a brown shirt and pants that are almost the same shade as his brown skin. His hair is long and soft, a hazel-colored cloud pulled into a large, fluffy bun at the crown of his head. He glares down at Henry with brown eyes, and her mouth still isn't able to form words. She breathes hard and shakes her head and hopes it looks apologetic.

The boy speaks, but Henry still can't understand. She doesn't think it's another language—it's just that the sound is garbled. Muffled. Fear must have scrambled her brain, and she must look confused, because the boy's glare softens. He reaches toward a bush—Henry notices then that there are lots of bushes around them—and plucks a red berry from its branch. He holds it out to her, and when she takes it, she holds it between two of her fingers, looking at him quizzically. He nods encouragingly, and though Henry doesn't recognize the berry (not a strawberry, not a raspberry) she puts it in her mouth, chews, and swallows.

When the boy speaks again, his voice is clear. It's like being on an airplane, the moment after you swallow to make your ears pop.

"You're new," the boy says gently.

"No, I live here," she answers.

The berry left a sweet, tangy taste on her tongue. She thinks her voice sounds like her legs feel. She checks over her shoulder, just to be sure the creature is gone.

"I'm not a big hiker," she says. "I used to go with my dad when I was younger. But never by myself. And this time I fell...and there was this animal...and it chased me...."

"Oh, you were hiking," he says. He tilts his head, curious and sympathetic. "I'm sorry. That's rough. Sometimes you think you know a place so well, and...well, it's like the trees grow legs, isn't it? Like they move around."

"I guess," Henry says. Her hands have stopped trembling. Her knees might take a little longer. "I stayed on the path until I fell. A sinkhole, I think. I still don't know how that...I mean, it was weird. A cave but not..."

"A lot of people get lost in caves," he says, and Henry knows he doesn't know, so she can't be mad at him, but her stomach clenches anyway. *Cave* has become almost like a swear word since her father disappeared.

"But it was more like a tunnel...," she starts, then stops. It's all begun to feel a little impossible, and she wonders if she hit her head. She's relieved she found a person.

"Are you okay?" the boy asks.

"Something chased me," she says. "It wasn't a bear or a mountain lion. It was huge...and white...I've never seen anything like it...."

"White?" he says, frowning. "I've never seen anything like that in there. It must have been on your side."

"Huh?"

"What did it look like?"

"It was like if you mixed a polar bear and a dinosaur together."

He smiles a strange smile.

"Dinosaurs," he says. "I think I remember those."

"Huh?"

"Nothing. It's just been a while since I thought about dinosaurs," he says.

"Oh." Henry still feels like she's on the Ferris wheel, even if it has slowed down. She considers that she imagined the animal. *Did* she hit her head when she fell? She decides to focus on the boy. "I'm sorry I ran into you. I wasn't paying attention."

"That's kind of how it happens sometimes," he says, and Henry doesn't know what he means, but he's shrugging and leaning down to pick up a bucket. She realizes now that when she ran into him, he spilled it.

"Oh, I'm sorry," she cries, and finds the strength to haul herself up from the ground. "Let me help."

"All right," he says.

He's been picking berries. The bucket is still half full. The rest are on the grass around him.

"Sorry," she says again.

"It wasn't your fault."

"What kind of berries are these?" She holds one up,

58

peering at it. They're round and red, like the ones on Christmas holly.

"They're called makab." He pauses and looks at her quickly. "Please don't tell anyone about these bushes, by the way. I just found this cluster this morning, and people have a habit of hoarding them. But then they just go bad. No one needs more than a few. I just get a basket sometimes to trade."

"Oh, okay." She drops the berry into the bucket. "Trading for what?"

"Just about everything."

He looks at her again, longer this time. She gets the feeling that there's something he's waiting for her to say.

"Do you know how close we are to Wade Road?" she asks. "It's over by Stuart Middle."

He looks down at his berries, gathering up a last few handfuls.

"Ahh … no, I don't know where that is," he says.

Once, on a first day of school, Henry sat in the wrong homeroom for twenty minutes. She felt the teacher looking at her, checking the class list. Even before she knew something was wrong, she knew something was wrong. This feels like that.

"Do you, um, have a phone, then?" she asks. "That I could borrow? I don't really know how I ended up here, but I don't want to go back in the woods and get lost…."

The boy sighs then—a long, tired sound. He picks up the bucket and stands, and only then does he make eye contact again. He looks sad.

"Um, I'm sorry, but... you already are."

"What?"

"You're, um, already lost," he says. He walks a few feet to where a smaller bucket is sitting and picks that up too. "You should probably walk down the hill with me."

Henry thinks this conversation feels very strange. There are more questions she would like to ask, but the boy has already turned away and is making his way among the bushes. Henry doesn't see a path, but he seems to know where he's going.

"You know the way?" she calls after him. "You won't get lost too?"

The boy pauses, considering. Then he looks back over his shoulder at her, and he smiles, even if his eyes are still a little sad.

"Not here," he says, then keeps walking, and Henry doesn't have much of a choice but to follow.

CHAPTER 7

Henry knows for sure that something strange is happening when they reach the bluffs that jut out from the forest, overlooking a town she has never seen before. The roofs down below look like round rocks covered in a layer of moss, and then there are some longer buildings clustered together, corner to corner, in a rough-edged circle. Among them all are what seem like scatterings of white stones, some of them as large as boulders, like someone took a rice cracker and crushed it in their fist before sprinkling the pieces over the town. Smoke rises in gray smudges from some houses' chimneys, and when Henry follows the smoke with her eyes, she sees the water. Lots and lots of it. An ocean where an ocean should not be.

"Um, what is that? Is that a lake? Where...?"

She trails off, taking in the water's bigness. It's almost a blue-gray wall between them and the horizon. At its edge are docked ships of all kinds. Tall ones with towering masts that remind her of pirate ships from the movies; smaller sailboats with brightly colored sails; short fat boats like the ones Henry has seen fishing on the river she and Ibtihaj cross over on the way to the library. But she's been crossing the river all her life, and she's never heard of it leading to this.

"It's not a lake," the boy says quietly.

"What do you mean?"

"It's called the Pepper Sea," he says.

Henry has never heard of an inland sea near Ripling. Her teacher last year, Mrs. Parker, gave them many map tests, and she would have made sure it was on at least one of them. Henry is good at tests. She would remember a Pepper Sea. She wonders if the boy is joking, so she asks him, very carefully.

"Joking about what?" he asks.

"About . . . that. The Pepper Sea."

"We should keep moving," he says as an answer. He gazes off toward the so-called sea. Henry notices for the first time the far-off dark clouds, high up. It's the kind of sky that promises a night of storms. She wonders if that's what the boy is worried about.

"I just need to call my parents, I'm sorry," she tells him. "I don't have a phone."

"Let's just get down the hill."

Henry doesn't like asking questions. Each one feels like pulling her own teeth. But the boy keeps dodging the non-questions. She has to ask outright.

"Okay, but ... do you have a phone?"

"I'd rather you come down and talk to Angie."

"Angie?"

"Yes."

Henry wishes she hadn't bumped into him. The water that he calls the Pepper Sea seems bigger every time she looks at it.

"Okay, then," she says. And then after a second, adds: "Sorry."

"You say sorry a lot," he mumbles, continuing down the path.

Henry feels her face get hot.

"I'm Wolfson," he says. It almost sounds like an apology of its own.

"Wolfson?"

"Yes."

"Oh. I'm Henry."

"Hi, Henry."

"Hi."

Henry notices that the ground has begun to level out, and when she and Wolfson get down to the very bottom, she pauses and looks back up toward where they came from. At the top,

Quinvandel looms like a green storm cloud. It looks different than it does from her backyard. Taller. Denser. Not exactly scary, but like someone has put an Instagram filter over it. So many unasked questions in her mind. *Who is Angie? What town is this? Am I safe here?*

"Are you okay?" he asks.

"I just don't like not knowing where I am."

"Angie will help."

"Who is Angie?"

"Angie is who I take my makab to," he says. "And she's been here a long time. Folks usually bring new people to her too."

"Does she have a phone?"

He glances at her sideways.

"I'll let you ask her."

They've reached level ground—it's a straight walk to the town Henry doesn't recognize. Now that they're closer she can smell food, smoky and spicy and sweet. But her stomach is still full of the bean pie Ibtihaj and her family made. She wonders how she can have ended up all the way in another town when she hasn't yet digested her pie.

In the distance she hears the squawky calls of seabirds.

"I don't think I've ever seen a seagull within a hundred miles of here," she says.

"Uh, there are lots of birds here. Gulls too."

She glances at him.

"I've never met someone named Wolfson."

"Oh," he says. "It's pretty simple. Son of wolves."

"...son of wolves."

"I was adopted."

Henry can now hear what sounds like a market. People talking, the sounds of birds and business. Someone chopping wood. She finds herself listening for the rhythm of the ocean. *But that can't be the ocean*, she reminds herself. It doesn't make sense. She hears a cat meowing, a falling axe, and then the rushing of wind.

"Duck!" someone screams, and if it wasn't for the shadow swooping down, Henry probably wouldn't have. The word *duck* doesn't truly sink into her ear until she's flat on the ground, the gust of the thing that just flew over her shifting her hair.

"Wolfson! In here!" the same someone cries.

There's a girl standing in the doorway of a shed a few feet away. She has deep brown skin and holds a broom like a sword.

"Ndidi!" Wolfson calls. "Are you okay?"

"Yes, but get in here o! They're coming back around!"

"Let's go," Wolfson says, and leaps up. Henry scrambles to follow him. Her mind fills with the white beast from the forest. Has it followed her here? On *wings*?

"Quickly!" the girl called Ndidi shouts. Henry can hear the swooping sound.

Henry dives into the shed where the girl stands in the door,

65

Wolfson one step behind. As soon as they're both inside, Ndidi uses the hand not holding the broom to slide the door closed with a whoosh. Outside, something bumps against it, hard enough to send a shiver through the small building. Henry backs as far away as she can, pressing against the wall. Dad would probably be outside taking pictures from a tree branch, but Henry wants to burrow into the wood of this shed.

"What's gotten into them?" Ndidi says.

"It's been getting worse," Wolfson says, shaking his head.

"What were those things?" Henry pants. "Vultures?"

"Bats," Wolfson says.

"*Bats?*"

"Yes. They've been behaving strangely," Ndidi adds, with her eye to a crack in the door.

"But...they were huge. When it flew over my head..."

"They're not like that at home?" Wolfson asks, eyebrows raised.

"These are like tourist airplanes," Ndidi says. "Yes, much bigger than home."

She turns and looks at Henry for the first time, studying her. Ndidi has a round, soft face like a baby's, but with a concentrated worry line between her eyes.

"Hi, I'm Ndidi."

"I'm Henry."

"You're okay?" Wolfson asks.

"Yes." Ndidi nods. "I came in here to get jam for Javier, and when the bats saw the door open, they came right for it. They're hungry, maybe?"

"I don't know if they get hungry."

"But why are they so big?" Henry presses. "How?"

"Why is anything the way it is here?" Ndidi says with a shrug.

Where is here? Henry thinks.

"You okay?" Ndidi asks.

"She's new," Wolfson says quickly.

Henry shoots a look between them.

"I'm not really *new*," she says carefully. "I'm just kind of turned around."

"Nno," Ndidi says. "Welcome anyway. Sorry about the bats. I don't think they're really after us; they've just been acting weird lately."

"I thought the weird part is that they're so huge."

"Well, that too. But things are different here."

"I noticed," Henry says. "Do you guys ever come to Ripling? That's my town. I'm trying to figure out how far I hiked."

"I've…um, never heard of it," Wolfson says. "Let's get going, okay?"

Henry wishes Ibtihaj were here with her. Henry is a good student, but Ibtihaj is a *very* good student. Dates, maps, history—all neatly organized file cabinets in her brain. Henry thinks her brain works more like her collages. She needs to gather many little pieces, and eventually she can put them together into a picture that makes sense. The picture she's putting together of this town isn't adding up into anything yet.

"I just saw Angie a few minutes ago," Ndidi says to Wolfson. She makes important eyes at him.

"At the market?"

"Yes. Is that where you're taking Henry?"

"Yeah."

"Good."

"What about the bats?" Henry says, just to say something. Right away she wishes she hadn't. What would her father have done if he'd seen them? More than try to film them, she thinks. Joseph Lightfoot is Discovery Joe. He is the man who sees buffalo on the plain and walks past the sign that says DO NOT APPROACH with his palms outstretched. Henry's cheeks burn, but no one notices.

Ndidi cracks the door and peeks out.

"It looks like they're all roosting in that tree," she says. "But as soon as we open this door, they'll probably swoop. You two ready to run?"

Wolfson nods, and so does Henry. Her heart feels like it's gliding on bat wings of its own—not a smooth flight but skittery and jagged. *But Dad would do this*, she thinks.

Ndidi throws open the door. When the light from outside

floods the small shed, a thought floods Henry. For once, she hadn't gone into Quinvandel to find her father. He was found. No, she had gone in to find something else. A piece of herself that looked like him, perhaps.

With this thought in her mind, she moves past Wolfson so that when Ndidi steps outside, Henry is stepping out with her.

This time the bats don't move. Some of them have buried their faces in their wings. *The sun is so bright*, Henry thinks. She feels sorry for the bats, fearsome as they are.

"Why don't they just go back to their cave?" she wonders out loud.

"Things have been strange," Ndidi says, shaking her head. "I've only been here a week or so, but every day it's something else. Yesterday a group of seals came ashore. The tides had stopped, you see. They were confused. Getting fish in still water is different than water with tides, I guess."

"No tides?"

"Not since I've been here. Look at the water."

The three of them had started walking from the shed toward the market, the Pepper Sea far ahead. If Ndidi hadn't mentioned it, Henry might not have noticed. But she sees that it's true. The water sits like a flat painting. She doesn't want to keep arguing that it can't be a sea.

"You've been here for a week?" she asks Ndidi instead. "Are you visiting family?"

Ndidi opens her mouth to answer, but then she shuts it again.

"There's Angie," she says, and points.

This is how asking questions always makes Henry feel. Like she stepped out onto a rope bridge and then one of the ropes broke. Not like she's falling, but like she's dangling.

But the market distracts her. When Wolfson said *market*, she had pictured the farmers market her mother goes to: a row or two of stalls, folding tables popped up with tomatoes and eggs and bunches of kale. But this feels like a town all by itself. Roofless, but the perimeter of the market is dotted with a bunch of thick-trunked trees. Their vines reach out and wrap around one another like good friends holding hands—Henry and the others have to duck under the vines to enter. She turns back to study the plants. They don't look like any she's ever seen in Quinvandel—their green is deep and wild and reminds her of a rainforest documentary. She thinks her father would know their names, even if he had never left the United States. She notices then how often she thinks of what her father would know, what he would do. Her stomach sinks. Her father being gone was like having a little bird sitting on her shoulder every day.

"The flower stall," Wolfson says. "Past the well."

Henry doesn't see the flower stall. She sees too many other things. Crowds of people, some wearing strange hats, some

70

carrying buckets of water on their heads. Many of them are going either to or from a well that sits in the shade between two thick trees at the center of the market. It's by the well that Henry notices a llama carrying a bucket of water on either side of its body, strapped across a saddle pad. But no one is leading the llama—it walks by itself. It gives the impression that it went for its own water. A smaller llama tags along behind it, hop-skipping.

"What is...?" Henry starts, but fades off, because she's not sure what she actually wants to ask. A feeling is stirring. Déjà vu, her mother would call it, but not quite. What did her father say? A place where children roam with deer? But...

"It's already busy," Wolfson remarks. "I'm glad we got here early."

"I never noticed that rope," Ndidi says, pointing. "What is that?"

Wolfson follows her finger, and so does Henry. Two big thick ropes, as big around as Henry's arm, are bolted to the ground in the clearing of the market. Alongside them, a metal structure that reminds Henry of a merry-go-round or a wind-mill laid on its side. The ropes attached to the bolt cut through the clear sky, taut. They arrow off into the sky, toward the mountain. So far, Henry can't make out where they end.

"I don't know," Wolfson says. "It's been there as long as I've been here. Someone said maybe it was used to transport things to the top of the mountain—like you turn the wheel and there's a pulley way up there somewhere. But no one goes there."

Henry follows the other two wordlessly, winding through the market with her mouth half-open. She can't stop swiveling her head. So many people, and none of them look like home. Not that everyone in Ripling looks the same, but there's a certain way people are there. The teenagers wearing Supreme. The parents in cargo pants. Everyone moving unhurriedly in the aisles of the grocery store. Not here. It's not just that everyone looks so different, but it's also that no one is together. In Ripling, if Henry went to a farmers market, she would find clusters of families. Kids who look something like their parents. Families have a certain look, and no one here does, even if everyone is dressed mostly the same. All these people—the same-color cloth on top and bottom, some of them walking from stall to stall, some just standing and looking around—even the ones talking to one another, seem separate. Like fireflies in a field.

And then there are the animals. It's not just the llamas: Henry sees horses, cats, a peacock, and several dogs, including a couple of big ones that look suspiciously like wolves. But no one gives them a second glance, although (like the other animals) they don't seem to belong to anyone.

"What *is* this place?" she says. The weirdness is beginning to stack up.

Her question seems to make Wolfson walk faster.

"Almost there," he says, and closes the gap between them and a stall where a small Black woman with close-cropped silver hair and a catlike face stands with her hands full of flowers. Her stall is a tiny shop entirely covered with blossoms, all of them the same soft purple. Some of them grow from pots, and others are hanging upside down from the roof slats, drying. Then there are lengths and lengths of them all woven together into daisy chains. The whole place gives off a soft, sweet smell. Angie is smiling and waving goodbye to another woman. Her smile grows even bigger when she sees Wolfson.

"Right on time, as always," she says. Her voice is deeper than Henry expected, and a little scratchy. It reminds Henry of a tiger purring. "You're the best berry hound in This Place. Where do you find so many? You still won't tell me?"

"No, ma'am," Wolfson says, and he grins, but it fades quickly. He glances at Henry. "Um..."

Angie looks at Henry, then back at Wolfson, then at Henry again. Her face changes, and Henry feels her own get hotter and hotter, knowing something is going on but not knowing what.

"Oh, hello," Angie says. The tiger in her voice is more like a house cat now. "You look like you need some help. What's your name? I'm Angie."

"Uh, Henry."

"How old are you?"

"Twelve." Henry has always been told not to give strangers personal information, and though she needs Angie's help, Henry tries to steer away from telling her anything else. "Do you have a phone? I got turned around in Quinvandel, and I need to call someone to come pick me up."

"Ah, honey," Angie says. Her eyes were so bright a moment ago, but now the sparkle seems to dim. "This is going to be tough, but I need to explain something to you."

If there is a meter in Henry's brain that measures "weird," it begins to tick into the red. Henry doesn't like how Angie is saying *honey*, or how Wolfson has stepped a little away, averting his eyes.

"I really just need a phone…," Henry starts, but Angie shakes her head.

"There are no phones here," she says. "This isn't home."

"I *know* it's not home," Henry says. "I need to *get* home."

"This is complicated," Angie says calmly. "But I'm going to explain it as simply as I know how. I've given this speech more times than you can imagine, so just let me tell you, okay? It's easier if you just listen for a minute."

"Um…"

"You got lost," Angie continues quickly. "In the forest, it sounds like. Quinvandel? I don't know that one, but maybe someone else around here does. We'll see. But you're not going to be able to get back there with a phone call, Henry. That doesn't work here. You're lost. But if it's any comfort, everyone here is and—"

"Everybody around here knows Quinvandel," Henry interrupts. "It borders pretty much everything in town, how can you not—"

"Because your town is far, far away," Angie says, interrupting Henry now. "Or maybe close but unreachable...no one really knows how it works. But you're lost, honey. We get all types here, in This Place. Hikers, sailors, people visiting new cities. Not just people either. Birds blow in from all over. Storms and such. Bears reintroduced from captivity..."

As if to make her point, a bear lumbers between Angie's stall and the next stall over, where a man selling bread gives the bear a friendly wave. Maybe Henry is imagining things, but she thinks the bear nods in response.

Henry *really* wishes Ibtihaj were here—she's so good at being logical. She always asks so many questions. Good ones. And Henry can rarely even manage one.

Wolfson and Ndidi have been listening from a safe distance, and when Henry looks at them she hopes they will start smiling, admit that this is a joke, pull an iPhone from

75

a pocket. But Wolfson's expression is only more uncomfortable. Ndidi gnaws on her lip. Wolfson hesitantly steps forward again.

"Listen," he says. "I know it's weird and hard to understand, but let me try to…ugh, I hate this part. Look, this is a place for lost people. People who get lost end up here. Not just 'Oh, I took a left instead of a right.' I mean *lost* lost. Some people stay a long time before they find their way, and some people are only here for a bit. It's different for everybody. And, you know, um, some people stay. They have their reasons. But we take care of each other, and you'll be safe."

It's the most words he's said in a row, and he looks a little exhausted.

"You'll be safe," Angie echoes. "You won't be on your own."

"None of this makes sense," Henry says, panicking. "Can you *please* just let me use the phone? My parents are going to start worrying and—and…"

She trails off, stammering, and for a moment sadness seems to overwhelm Angie's face.

"It's a terrible thing to lose a child," she says. She looks like she's sinking.

"It's going to be okay," Wolfson says, his voice cracking. "I can help you get used to it…I know it's weird…but it's not so bad here—"

"Here," Henry cries. "What is *here*? What are you guys even saying?"

"*Here* is This Place," he says. "That's...that's where you are."

"What are you telling me, this is another *planet*?" Henry's laugh is fake and weak. She wants so badly for one of them to say no.

"Maybe," Angie says. "We're not really sure, honestly. It's kind of...between places."

Henry begins to back away from them. "This is...No way."

"It's all right," Angie says. She doesn't call Henry closer, but she watches her carefully. "I know this seems impossible. So for now, just try looking up."

Henry stares at her for what feels like a long time. Nearby, a camel walks leisurely past, all by itself, chewing cud. Henry gapes at it. Then slowly, slowly she lifts her chin to look at the sky.

At first, all Henry sees are the branches and vines that stretch over parts of the market. But beyond them is the pale blue sky. At its top is the sun. And another sun too.

Two suns, staring down like two blazing eyes.

CHAPTER 8

Henry runs.

She startles the camel, but she doesn't care or stop. She dodges around people and animals and between trees, and she sprints past the well. A few people shout, and Wolfson or Angie might be one of them, but Henry doesn't look back. Her legs go and go. They carry her under the vines and out into the open meadow, where she pauses, panting. There are more people walking to the market, some carrying baskets, some carrying buckets. None of them give her a second glance. They don't look like anyone Henry has ever seen: no familiar faces from the grocery store or people from school's parents.

"I was only in Quinvandel for twenty minutes," she

whispers. "This makes no sense. It would take me longer than that to walk to school...."

She hears the calling of the gulls and glances up, but before she sees the birds she sees the two suns again. She slaps her palms over her eyes.

"No way. No *way*."

This time when she runs, she angles toward the lake. The "Pepper Sea." There must be a sign, the way there are signs at the front of parks and forest reserves. Something that will both tell her where she is and prove that this isn't what Wolfson and Angie say it is.

But when Henry gets to the lake, she hits sand. It's white and powdery and sifts into her shoes. Not a sign to be seen, even when she cups a hand over her eyes and looks up and down the beach. All the boats sit silently. Schooners, fishing boats, and many canoes and kayaks, some of them overturned and broken. The water is so still Henry thinks she could walk on it. Far off in the sky over the water are dark, heavy clouds.

She wanders to the edge of the lake. How to tell if a body of water is actually an ocean or a lake? She's visited Chicago and seen Lake Michigan—if she didn't know, she would have thought it was an ocean. It just wasn't salty.

Henry hesitates, then crouches down to poke one finger into the water. Then she puts it quickly into her mouth.

Salt. So strong it makes her spit.

The dizziness swoops down like one of the bats, and the next thing she knows she's sitting in the sand, swaying. Out of the corner of her eye, she sees something move, and it occurs to Henry that she's too dizzy to run again, that this might be the end. But it's only a crab. It's as big as her hand and shiny black, with a pattern of white dots along its shell.

"Oh, hi," she says softly, admiring it. She's never seen a crab like this and wonders if anyone has. For a moment, she forgets about being lost and imagines taking it home to show her parents. Imagines holding it on the cover of *National Geographic* magazine, her father proud and grinning.

The crab has a stick in its claw and drags it through the sand. Henry watches in awe. Is it building a nest? She's been to an ocean beach only once or twice, and the crabs always scuttled away when anyone came close. It goes on dragging the stick through the sand, and Henry goes on watching, until she slowly starts to realize.

"No way...," she whispers.

The crab drags the stick a few more inches, its delicate black legs sidling through the sand. When it's finished, its claw releases the stick into the ocean. Then it stands waiting.

There in the sand, etched carefully by the crab, is the word *HELLO*.

Henry buries her face in her hands. She doesn't know if she's going to cry or scream, but in the end it's neither. She sits there, hiding from the suns, from the crab, and this impossible ocean. She sits and sits and sits. She sits so long her butt goes to sleep. She sits until eventually someone gently touches her shoulder. A human hand, not a crab claw.

It's Ndidi.

"I'm sorry," Ndidi says.

Henry doesn't answer. She rests her chin on her pulled-up knees and stares out at the water.

"Sha, scoot back at least," Ndidi says gently. "There's no tide right now. But everything has been very unpredictable. Better to be safe."

Henry still doesn't speak, but she lifts up on her hands and scuttles backward like the crab would. She wishes there was a tide so it could wash over the etched *HELLO*.

"A crab wrote that," Henry says, pointing. "Did you know that?"

"Nothing will surprise me now. Not in This Place."

"This place," Henry repeats.

"It is hard to believe, but it's true. You get used to it o. And who knows, you may not be here very long. There was a girl who was here for two days."

This interests Henry.

"How did she leave?"

Ndidi curls her knees to her chest too. She wears pale pink shorts and a shirt of the same color. Just like everyone else in the market: clothes of the same knit, the same color on top and bottom.

"I don't know," she answers. "No one knows about anyone else when it comes to finding their way out. There's one person who has been here twice, though. Can you believe that? Letting yourself get lost once, lost enough to end up here, then getting lost a second time? Sha, if I ever get home, I might never leave my parents' house again."

"Are you from around here? Close to Ripling?"

She raises an eyebrow.

"I am from Abuja."

Henry looks at her blankly. Ndidi smiles gently.

"Do they not teach world geography in your American schools? Abuja. It is in Nigeria."

Henry jerks her head up.

"Are you telling me you ended up here from *Nigeria*? Africa?"

"That is where I'm *from*," Ndidi corrects. "I got lost in Cape Town."

"South Africa," Henry says slowly. "Cape Town is a city, right?"

"You know *that* one o," she says, and rolls her eyes a little. Then smiles, like the sarcasm has embarrassed her and not Henry.

The two girls sit silently. Above them the two suns burn

on, but Henry refuses to look at them. She doesn't want to see them and covers her eyes again. She doesn't want to see any of this. Ndidi isn't lying. How could she be? For what reason? The truth is impossible, but here Henry sits.

"It's hard," Ndidi says after a while. When Henry looks at her, her chin is resting on her knees, her eyes staring out at the sea. "Like being in prison, maybe. I want to go home. But I must not want it badly enough, hmm?" She pauses, quiet. "But wanting can't have much to do with it, or this place would be empty. Everybody here *wants* to go home. Well, almost everybody."

"Who *doesn't* want to?" Henry asks, shocked.

"Wolfson, I think." She shrugs. "He's been here since he was a baby. I think this *is* home for him now."

"He came here when he was a *baby?*" Henry cries. "He got lost as a baby?"

"It happens more than you think," someone says from behind them, and Henry and Ndidi both jump.

It's Wolfson. He stands at the edge of the sand, one bucket in each hand, both of them empty now. Ndidi looks pained.

"Sorry o," she says. "Wasn't trying to tell your business."

But Wolfson only shrugs.

"I don't mind," he says. "Henry, you should come on. Angie wants me to help you get settled in."

Henry thinks this feels like some sort of messed-up camp.

"Are there, like, tents?" she asks.

"Tents." Ndidi laughs. She hauls herself up from the sand. "No, not tents. You'll sleep at the hostel with me."

"What about you?" Henry asks Wolfson.

"He lives with his parents."

"But..."

"I told you I was adopted," he says. "I was adopted here."

"Let's stop by your house first," Ndidi says, grinning. "You can drop off your buckets."

The three of them pick their way across the sand, Ndidi pointing things out to Henry: beehives, nesting pelicans, and all the many kites and balloons in trees that Ndidi says end up in This Place regularly before eventually disappearing.

"What do you think?" she says after she's pointed out a tree decorated with hundreds of umbrellas. "Makes no sense, does it?"

"So everything lost ends up here?" Henry asks. Believing it all is like wading into a pool. First her toes, then her ankles. Back in Ripling, the pool opens in June but is never warm enough to swim in without shivering until August. Then it closes just when everyone has gotten used to the water. But Henry doesn't want to get used to This Place.

"Can't be *everything*," Ndidi says thoughtfully. "It would be too much. And I never find things like money here. People lose money all the time. I don't see piles of it anywhere."

"Maybe someone else always finds it too fast," Henry offers.

Ndidi shrugs. Wolfson just keeps walking quietly beside them.

"Where do your parents live?" Henry asks him.

"You don't see the house?" Ndidi says, but she grins shyly, a gentle trickster, and Henry squints around them. They'd left a meadow a few minutes ago and ended up on a different path into more forest. It's not the dense stuff like where Henry met Wolfson—it's paler green with many white-trunked birches, hills of stone just off the path. Henry doesn't see a house anywhere.

Wolfson almost looks like he's going to smile, and though everything is strange and Henry still thinks she might be dreaming, she wants to smile too. But then his almost-smile folds down into a frown.

"Something's wrong," he says. And before Henry or Ndidi can say anything, he's dropped the buckets and sprinted ahead on the path.

Henry is still looking for a house when he darts sideways off the path and into the trees, and by the time she catches up she finds him already disappearing into a hole in the stone. A cave. Ndidi plunges in behind him, and though *cave* still makes her shiver, so does Henry.

They have to crouch low to get through the opening, but

once inside Henry is surprised to find it airy and smooth. It smells dry and clean, like sun on cedar. It's a home: There are rugs and baskets and ivy on the walls. It's beautiful.

But it's also, she sees, a mess.

Many of the baskets are overturned, cushions are ripped, and apples roll freely across the stone floor. Chairs are flipped over. Wolfson is in the corner, bending over a pile of blankets, something cradled in his arms.

It's a puppy.

"Oh no," Ndidi gasps. Her hands are clutched over her mouth, and she gasps again, sharper this time, when Wolfson's hand comes away from the puppy red with blood. "Oh no, oh no. Is she dead? She cannot be dead."

"No," Wolfson murmurs. He clutches the puppy, silver-and-white fur blowing under his breath, holding her against his chest.

"What happened?" Henry breathes.

Bats, says a voice. She turns to see who has come in behind them.

And she finds two wolves, heads low and eyes blazing.

Henry doesn't scream. Instead she just says "*Oh*" and then says "*Oh*" again, and grips Ndidi's shoulder, trying to pull her away to safety, wherever that is. But Ndidi's hand rests on top of Henry's and gently pulls it away.

"Sha, relax," she says. "They won't hurt you."

Ndidi turns to the wolves and says apologetically, "She's new."

But the wolves ignore them both, their great furry bodies arrowing over to where Wolfson kneels, cradling the puppy. *A wolf puppy*, Henry realizes. Wolfson gently holds her out to the wolves, who inspect her with noses and tongues. Like the pup, they are silver, black, and white, one with copper combed through the length of their back and shoulders.

It's just a scratch on her head, one of them says. It takes a long moment for Henry to realize that she's not hearing the wolf in her ears but *between* her ears. The voice is obviously coming from the wolf, and Ndidi hears it, too, but the sound isn't in the room of the cave. It's inside Henry's head.

Ndidi glances at Henry, then glances again.

"You'll need to eat the makab berry every day or so until you settle in. Otherwise you won't be able to understand anyone."

But Wolfson interrupts, talking to the wolves.

"How could it be bats?" he asks. "They've never bothered us before."

They are confused, the copper-streaked wolf says. *I believe they were looking for a place to roost. We chased them off, but they were already frightened before they saw us.*

Wolfson holds his cheek to the whimpering puppy.

"Why is this happening?" he says quietly.

Things are strange, the other wolf says. *Something is wrong in This Place. I wish I knew what it was.*

Wolfson goes on stroking the wolf pup, whispering something down to her. He looks up and finds Henry staring.

"Oh," he says. "Sorry. Henry, this is my sister, Daughter. These are my parents."

He nods at the wolves. They both turn to look at Henry, eyes yellow amber and piercing.

"Um, hi," Henry says, and they each incline their head before turning back to their cub. Or cubs, she guesses. One human, one wolf.

I do not think the bats meant to hurt her, one of the wolf parents says. *The bats are as confused as we are.*

You should get to the hostel, the other says, turning to Ndidi and Henry. *It will be dark soon. If they are behaving this way in the light, I have worries about the dark.*

"Yes, let's go," Ndidi agrees. She looks at Wolfson. "Do you still want to walk with us to the hostel?"

"I should probably stay here," he says, frowning down at his sister.

Go, one of his parents says. *With the bats behaving oddly, it's better to be in a group. Stay at the hostel tonight—there are doors there, at least.*

"I've slept here my whole life," Wolfson says, his frown deepening. "I don't need a door."

The children at the hostel may need your calm more than two old dogs do, the copper wolf says gently. *Leave Daughter to us.*

"You're not old," Wolfson grumbles, and he tenderly places the wolf pup into the nest of blankets, squishing them around her. "And you're not dogs."

Ndidi and Henry wait while Wolfson retrieves the buckets and takes them inside the den, then hugs each of his parents around the neck. Henry is a little envious of that, how at ease the boy is around two massive wolves. At home she has seen only coyotes, which she's been afraid of since they ate a neighbor's Yorkie. These wolves are three times a coyote's size. But now that Henry knows how gentle their voices are, she thinks it's hard to look at them the same way.

"How...how do they talk?" Henry asks when the three of them are walking again, and when they're far enough away from the den that she doesn't think the wolves will overhear.

Henry looks at Ndidi for the answer because, though she's a little shy, she's generally more talkative than Wolfson, but Ndidi shrugs.

"I'm not the one to ask o. Wolfson has been here the longest of all the kids."

"I don't know either," he says, ducking under a low branch. "Angie explained what she knew when I got old enough, and she's been here longest. But what she knows is what someone else told her. Basically: No one can understand anyone when they first get here. The makab berry seems to help right away, and you need to eat it a few times until you're settled. Then everyone seems to just understand each other. Including the animals."

"Just thought of something," Ndidi says. "Has anyone *asked* the bats what the problem is?"

"Well, that's the thing," Wolfson says. "From what Angie says, she was told the bats were here before anyone else. Some other animals too. They might be able to talk, but if they do, they only talk to each other."

"Were they here before the witch?" Ndidi asks.

"The witch?" Henry asks. "What witch?"

"People say there's a witch here that hides in the forest. No one has ever seen her, and I don't know if the rumors are true," Wolfson says. "But maybe the bats came with her. I don't know."

They walk in silence, but Henry's mind is still on the den.

"So...you were adopted?" she says after a while. She wonders if it's rude to act like a boy being raised by wolves is unusual. It's usual here. But Wolfson doesn't act offended; he only sighs.

"Yeah. Mother and Father took me in when I first got here. I was scared of other people, they say. I don't really remember a whole lot from then. I was little."

"You don't remember where you came from?" Henry asks.

"Kind of. A traveler got lost a few years ago and helped me put the pieces together. Based on my memory of a river and a bridge and some other stuff, he thinks I'm from somewhere in Indiana. That's a place, I guess."

Henry nods, amazed and sad.

"Yes," she says. "A state. Not too far from me."

"America," Ndidi teases. "Sha, no wonder you don't go back, Wolfson."

He smiles, shaking his head.

"I don't know," he says. "I'm just...I'm fine here. All my memories before This Place are bad, so...why would I want to find my way back?"

"What do you remember?" Henry asks. Ndidi looks like she wishes she hadn't, and Wolfson notices.

"It's okay," he says. "I just remember a woman—my mom, I think. Hair like you, skin like you," he says to Henry. "And her mother too. They were always screaming. At each other. At me."

He stops talking and blinks many times in a row. The three of them have stepped out from the forest now and are back in the meadow. Ahead is the market, and Wolfson looks in its direction, but Henry thinks he's really looking far away.

"Sometimes I remember things." He shrugs. "Then it goes away. Like coins in the bottom of a well. Sometimes the sun lands on one just right. Sometimes there's only shadow. But they weren't kind people. Mother and Father have always been kinder. Here."

Henry doesn't feel dizzy anymore. What she feels instead is worse. Like the grim silence after the tornado siren goes off. The water of a swamp just after an alligator's tail slips back in. She feels still and quiet, and she thinks maybe this is just how it feels: knowing this is all real.

Up ahead people are still milling in and out of the market, and beyond it are the houses Henry saw from the mountain. Mostly short and round, but a few taller, two or three stories, which peek over the top of the market. She can make out some people in a few of the windows. They look out toward the ocean. The Pepper Sea.

"How did you get lost?" she asks Wolfson.

"We lived near some woods. I think I wandered in one day and never came out. I don't know if they even looked for me."

Henry stops midstride. She learned in school that Isaac Newton wrote the law of gravity after an apple fell onto his head. They're in the meadow, nothing overhead, but she feels as if something has struck her. A realization. Something true.

Her father was here in This Place.

She turns toward the Pepper Sea. All the people she can see on the beach, wandering the sand or standing with their toes in the still water. *They're all lost*, she thinks. It's impossible that they've all come from different places and still all ended up here, but here they all are. Her father must have been one of them.

"Are you all right?" Ndidi says. She and Wolfson have stopped next to her, both looking worried.

"I...I..."

The time between Henry's eleventh birthday and her twelfth birthday was one year but felt like one hundred, and in those hundred years she had wondered but never said it out loud: What if her father just wanted to leave them? At night when Henry went to sleep without him in their house, she imagined him on a grand adventure without her and her mother. But he hadn't been.

He'd been stuck here.

"Henry?" Wolfson says. He looks at her the way he was looking at his wolf sister. Ndidi has extended her hands like she might catch Henry if she faints.

"What's the matter?"

But Henry can't tell them. The embarrassment is too much. She thinks of what Ndidi said about the only person in This Place who got lost twice. *Can you believe that? Letting yourself get lost once, lost enough to end up here, then getting lost a second time?* Henry thinks what their faces would look like if she told them her father got lost in the woods and then Henry went into the very same trees after he'd emerged. She can't make herself say it out loud.

"I just..." She pauses. She can't. "I just can't believe this place is real."

Their faces relax. Ndidi's hands slowly sink to her sides.

"I don't know what real is anymore," she says. "But... ebezina. We're here now."

CHAPTER 9

There's an empty bed in Ndidi's room at the hostel, and when Henry walks in, Henry's name is written on the wall in chalk.

"You can sleep there," Ndidi says. "Fatimah was there, but she found her way last week. She was the one who found her way in two days. Lucky."

"When did you do that?" Henry says, still looking at her chalked name.

"It wasn't me o. It just comes. And goes. That's how you know if someone is just taking a walk or if they find their way. When Fatimah found her way, her name just faded right off the wall."

At the foot of the low bed is a basket, and inside is a blanket folded neatly. When Henry reaches down to touch it, it smells like soap and lilacs. She floats it down over the bed so she doesn't have to look at Ndidi or Wolfson, who leans against the doorframe.

"How does it work?" She can't help but ask, even if there's no answer. She's asking for herself, but she's asking for her father too. If he was here, how did he leave? She could still tell them about him. But then, she thinks, they'd wonder why she didn't say anything sooner.

"Dunno," Ndidi says. "Maybe the witch?"

"Angie says everybody finds their own way in their own way," Wolfson says. He doesn't seem to approve of the idea of a witch. "I've seen a lot of people come and go. No way is ever the same."

Henry wonders what her father's way was. And why did it take so long? She continues studying the room, thinking about where he might have slept. Draped over the window are several long chains of purple flowers, all woven together.

"Did Angie make those?" she asks, pointing.

"Yes," answers Wolfson. "She makes new ones all the time. Those flowers didn't start growing until she came, I've heard. Now she makes sure all the rooms have them so when people get here they feel more at home."

A tall white girl, older than them, appears in the doorway. She carries a basket full of bowls and brushes.

"Need help on the roof if you're all free," she says. "That storm that's been sitting over the sea is coming closer. Angie thinks it will hit tonight. We need to patch a few holes."

Ndidi stands, so Henry does too. They follow the older girl down the hallway, back toward where the ramp brought them up to the second floor. The hallways feel like inside and outside at the same time: protected, but with soft green moss growing on the walls. The ramps slope up gently, bare along the paths where people walk the most.

"Olga, is Angie worried about this storm?" Ndidi asks the older girl.

"Not too much," Olga calls over her shoulder. "I think she's more worried that it *won't* come and will just keep sitting out there."

"Is Angie the boss?" Henry asks as they all turn to troop up the last ramp.

"No boss here," Wolfson says. "Angie just knows a lot. She's seen it all."

"Except for this storm," Ndidi says, and even if Angie isn't worried, Henry can tell Ndidi is.

"Do *you* think it will be bad?" she asks.

They step up onto the roof, and all eyes drift to the sky

over the Pepper Sea. The dark mass of clouds looks no closer to Henry, but it does look darker. From up here she can see all the way to the market and its surrounding trees, where the shapes of bats still hang down.

"I don't know what to think," Ndidi says. She glances at Wolfson, looking expectant.

"I don't know." He sighs and adds reluctantly: "But everything has been weird lately. The bats. The storm. And snow."

"And this place is weird already," Ndidi mutters. "By definition o!"

"What snow?" Henry asks.

"It snowed three days ago," Ndidi says, half smiling. "It was a little pretty."

"It never snows here," Wolfson says firmly. "Not once my whole life."

"Come on," Olga calls from the other side of the roof. A few other people have appeared from the ramp. Everyone seems to know that they need to pitch in. Henry thinks maybe that's the thing about being lost—what else are you going to do?

They patch holes, crouching with pots of resin. Wolfson shows Henry and Ndidi how to use heavy wooden spatulas and brushes to smear the resin over gaps in the roof. When he moves off to help others, Henry crab-walks along the strip of roof Olga pointed her toward, Ndidi at her side. They work quietly. Henry never feels like she knows when it's the right time to talk. It got even worse after her father disappeared. Her mother was often silent, and all Henry's words felt like interruptions. Like her mother was always listening for her father to open the door, and Henry's voice made it too hard to hear.

"What are you thinking about?" Ndidi asks.

"My mom."

"Yes," Ndidi says. "I miss mine. I worry about her."

"She's worried about you."

"That's why I worry about her," she says quietly.

Henry nods. The resin on the roof looks shiny and hard as it dries, like frozen syrup.

"I just wonder... have they noticed I'm gone yet?" Henry says. "My uncle was asleep when I went out...."

The embarrassment that made her lie to Wolfson and Ndidi about her father gets stronger. What will her mother think? Henry imagines her mother answering the call confirming that one loved one came back from the forest, but another went in. Henry knows what it's like when someone goes missing. The search parties. The maps. They never found her father. And they won't find her either. She rests her hand against the waist belt she brought with her, the one that was her father's. Inside is the map of Quinvandel. She thinks about that and not the lump in her throat.

"Storm's swelling," someone with a deep voice calls. It's a copper-skinned man wearing pale pink on top and bottom. He carries a pot of resin in one hand and shades his eyes with his other, peering out at the Pepper Sea. "Finish up if you haven't. Don't forget that Mr. Felipe is bringing his telescope over after dinner. Angie finally found a piece to fix it over at Christopher's. So we're all going to take a closer look at that storm."

A few cheers go up. Henry has been focused on talking to Ndidi and patching holes—she didn't notice how many people had come up to the roof. Most of them are children. An older boy is carrying a baby. Maybe it's the smell of the resin—strong and smoky—but she feels sick.

"You're looking at the baby," Ndidi says, sitting back on her heels. "Even younger than when Wolfson got here. It's the saddest thing in the world, isn't it?"

Henry can only nod.

"How is a baby supposed to find its way?" Ndidi says, standing up and wiping her hands. "Not fair."

"How does this place even work?" Henry says. "There's no way all the lost kids in the world fit in this hostel."

"Well, people come and go every day." Ndidi shrugs. Wolfson joins them with his pot and brush, and together they all stand looking out at the Pepper Sea. Ndidi nudges him. "How do you think it works? You're Angie's friend, aren't you? Is

100

this place like a mosquito net? Catching all the lost people in the world?"

"Angie has her ideas." He shrugs. "I have mine."

"Well?" Ndidi says, poking him.

"Angie thinks this isn't the only place like this—that there are others and where you end up is where you end up. Me... I don't know. I think not everybody who gets lost ends up here. Some are where they are—the woods, the desert. But somehow some people end up here. There's more than one kind of lost."

Henry frowns, thinking about that. She agrees there's more than one kind of lost—the three of them are proof. But Wolfson seems to mean something else. But before Henry can ask, someone calls, "Mr. Felipe is here! He has the telescope!"

A couple of the smaller children cheer, and everyone starts moving toward the ramp to go down. The clouds above look even more swollen. Henry doesn't know how anyone will see anything through a telescope in a storm. She takes one last look at the Pepper Sea, thinking of her father. She can't know for sure that he was here, but she feels it in her bones that he was. He was stuck here, trying to get home, trying to find his way. He did it.

And so, Henry thinks, can she.

CHAPTER 10

The cafeteria at Henry's school in Ripling had just one solid smell, everything muddied together: *food*. In the dining room of the hostel in This Place, she can smell the individual things. Onion. Garlic. Potato. Before her father disappeared, had they cooked? Small things. Defrost, brief sizzling. Homesickness snaps her, like rubbing her hands on carpet, then touching a doorknob. She wonders if Ibtihaj knows she's gone, and the feeling stings more sharply.

But it melts with a hunger pang—the last thing she ate was the bean pie before noon. Now it's almost sunset, and she has no idea if time works the same way in This Place, but she thinks it doesn't matter if she's hungry. Hunger is hunger.

"Do you want to help me clean up?" Ndidi says. She's

already moved over to a long wooden table and is gathering up scraps of onions. Some other kids are mixing and chopping things. "Mr. Javier can make anything. But if you have requests, you have to help out."

"Does this mean you requested something?" Henry asks, nodding at Ndidi's busy hands. Henry cups her palms so the other girl can sweep peels off the table into them.

"I almost always do," Ndidi admits. "His version of egusi soup isn't as good as my mum's, but it's still good good." She pauses, gazing over at the pots boiling over flames. "I miss home. I didn't have a chance to cook in Cape Town before I got lost. So this makes me think of Abuja, pounding cassava with my cousins and aunties. The yard would be filled with music and family and people shouting and laughing. Or sometimes just the sound of bugs singing. I'm the oldest. Always having to watch the little ones. I never thought I'd miss it this much."

Her voice has gotten softer and softer. Henry can barely hear her toward the end. She's been missing her father for a year. Not from a strange in-between world like this, but from her own home. She knows what missing feels like. She just nods and swallows the lump in her throat.

"What do you eat with egusi soup?"

"Well," Ndidi says, "I have to say it is not *really* egusi. They have onions and things here. But no melon, no bitter leaf, no crayfish. But Javier uses other things where it's similar. At home we would eat it with fufu, all of us together. Do you know fufu?"

Henry shakes her head.

"Well, I like egusi with fufu. Some people eat it with rice. I will eat anything with rice. There's no rice here."

She looks as sad about rice as she does about her family. Henry thinks again about cooking at home. The cooking happened together. The eating happened apart. Her father carrying food to the basement with his artifacts and his footage. Henry wonders if she will be here long enough to miss bean pie as much as Ndidi misses egusi and fufu. Listening to her talk makes Henry feel like she's empty in another way. Like Henry is missing things to miss.

"Here comes the rain," Javier calls over the sound of knives chopping and water boiling, and everyone stops to listen. It sweeps down over the windows in sheets, and though Henry wishes she were home, she's grateful that she's here, inside with other people, instead of out in Quinvandel in the dark wet. But even after they've all been sitting at the long tables for an hour, everyone talking and eating the not-quite egusi soup, the thunder doesn't come.

"Angie's here!" Wolfson says, sitting up straighter.

Everyone shouts hello as they're eating, and Angie shoves the door closed against the wind. She wears what looks like a rubbery poncho, and when she slings it off, it leaves a puddle by the door. She comes straight over to Wolfson.

"I'm glad you're here," she says. "I heard what happened at the den. Are you okay?"

"I'm fine, but they hurt Daughter. I don't think they meant to, though."

"I don't think they did either."

"What is going on with them?" Wolfson asks. "The bats?"

"I wish I could say," Angie says. Her frown was soft before, but now it deepens. "Things have been ... strange lately."

"I almost wish it would really storm just to get it over with," Olga says from next to Wolfson. She alternates between eating the soup—which came out more like stew—and gulping water from a quart-sized jar. The stew is spicy, and Ndidi has been laughing quietly since Olga's first bite.

"The clouds out over the sea haven't moved," Wolfson says.

"So where's the rain coming from, then?" Javier calls from the stove.

"I don't see any clouds over us at all." Wolfson stares out into the night, looking worried. "It's like the rain's coming from nowhere."

"That makes no sense," Ndidi says. She stands up and joins them at the window, peeking out. "But he's right. And the clouds out over the sea look even bigger."

"Mr. Felipe," calls Angie. "Can you go ahead and set up that telescope when you're through?"

"On it," Mr. Felipe says. He stands up from the table, brushing crumbs out of his beard, and everyone watches him eagerly.

"Do you need help, Mr. Felipe?" Ndidi asks.

"Sweet Ndidi." He smiles. "You're always the one to offer. No, thank you. I can manage."

Ndidi looks a little embarrassed. She takes a napkin and wipes the wet mouth of a little kid standing nearby. A moment later Mr. Felipe is peering through the eyepiece.

From where Henry is sitting, she can see his mouth when it turns down into a frown.

"What is it?" Wolfson says quickly.

Mr. Felipe pauses. "I . . . can't find the moon."

"The moon is up inna sky!" the little kid next to Ndidi shouts.

"Yes, Fredrick, it usually is," Mr. Felipe says, still peering. "But tonight . . . it appears . . . not to be."

"Not to be?" Angie says, sounding puzzled.

"It's just not there," Mr. Felipe says.

"The moon can't just disappear out of the sky," Olga says. She's moving toward the telescope like she's going to look for herself when Ndidi cries out. She's so close it makes Henry jerk.

"Did you see that?" Ndidi says shrilly. Wolfson had just begun to turn away from the window, but she grips his arm.

"What?" he says, turning back. "I don't see anything."

"Everyone back away from the windows," Angie says, raising her voice. "Now."

"What did you see?" Henry asks. Her heart has begun to beat faster.

"In the dark," Ndidi says, leaning closer to the window. "Out there by the market. Like a flash of light."

The sudden rumble of thunder growls from the sky through the ground, and every person in the dining hall jumps. Even Angie. The building shudders. At home Henry wouldn't be worried, but she wonders how old this building is. She's noticed it doesn't have electricity—Javier and some of the older kids lit torches when the suns began to go down. Some of the torches on the wall flicker from the thunder.

"I guess you saw lightning," Wolfson says, still peering out into the dark.

"Lightning isn't on the ground," Ndidi says, her voice trembling. She has already started to gather Fredrick and other little kids nearby, pulling them back into a corner. She moves like a mother, or an eldest daughter. But a few other people drift closer to the windows, curious, and that's when Henry sees it too: a glimpse of something white, slicing through the rainy gloom.

Real lightning cracks then, snapping through the sky and splitting a far-off tree. There are gasps, but the sound is swallowed by the next roll of thunder.

"It's gone now," Ndidi calls from where she's herding the little kids. "I don't see—"

CRASH.

When the glass breaks, everyone screams. Henry is still at the table, but she jumps up and back as shards of glass scatter. The sound of the storm rushes in, howling like werewolves, drowning out the sound of everyone screaming until all Henry hears is the roar of thunder.

And then she sees the beast.

The night is as black as a cave, and the beast is as white as the pale insects that live inside one. But the beast is not an insect. Its massive head fills the whole window, teeth starlit and snapping. White eyes roll in wide sockets, pale blue in the torchlight.

"Back! Back!" Angie screams. "Run!"

Everyone is screaming, Henry is screaming, and by the fireplace the three babies in high chairs wail, and the beast seems to hear, turning its shaggy head in their direction. Its pearlescent teeth twinkle. Henry is frozen, half out of her chair. From this frozen place, she sees Ndidi rush to the babies, and then a chair flies through the air.

It strikes the beast fully across the face, soundless until it hits the floor, one wooden leg cracking. It's only when the beast slowly turns its eyes on Wolfson that Henry realizes it was he who threw the chair. Angie stands ready with a wooden platter. She passes a torch to Wolfson and holds another herself.

"Wolfson, go with your friends, please," Angie hisses.

He shakes his head. But there are tears on his face, and his hands must shake, too, because the light from his torch wavers.

"Javier," Angie calls without looking, "help Ndidi with the babies!"

She throws the platter, aiming for the beast's eyes, but this time the creature is ready. It snaps its shining teeth, and the platter explodes into splinters. The beast and Angie move forward at the same time, the beast trying to get more of its body through the window and Angie waving the torch. Wolfson joins her, waving his as well.

"Out!" Angie screams, over and over. "Out! Out!"

"Help them!" Henry yells, at no one, at everyone, maybe at herself. But she can't move.

Ndidi gets the babies, she and Olga and a tall skinny white boy snatching them out of their seats and running for the stairs. The little kids are already ahead, halfway up. It's Javier who grabs two more torches and dashes up to join Angie and Wolfson before the pale beast, waving the torches back and forth and shouting.

The reflection of the fire turns the beast's eyes orange and flickering. Javier swings one of the torches in a powerful arc that almost grazes the creature's snout. It rears back, the bulk of it high above Javier and Wolfson, and for one long terrible moment Henry thinks it's going to pounce and crush them all.

But the monster lets out one long, ragged scream, and Henry thinks every hair on her body is coated in ice. Then it screams again before pulling back, sending more broken shards of glass showering to the floor. With the window empty of its body, the wind comes rushing in its place, and the torches that kept the beast back are blown out like birthday candles.

"More fire!" Javier shouts. "Light these back up! Rápidamente!"

At some point Henry pressed herself against the wall. Just by her shoulder is another torch, mounted. The nearness of the flames finally thaws at least a layer of the terror in her bones. Her hands shake, but she pulls the torch from its sconce. Then she persuades her wobbly legs to run to the window.

The wind catches the fire when she gets close, almost blowing it out, and somewhere outside she can hear the beast screaming. It sounds like two. It sounds like three. But she focuses her energy on the torch, turning her body to shield the fire. Wolfson meets her, fumbling with his own, and Javier

110

works with Angie to flip one of the long dining room tables to block the broken window.

It keeps out the wind but not the beast's screaming. They all huddle down, everyone shocked silent. Everyone except Angie, who says, "I'm going to check on the babies." She stands, but not before she wraps an arm around Wolfson's shoulders. She whispers something in his ear, and he nods quickly in reply. Whatever she said makes his shoulders relax and sink down. He sniffs.

Angie disappears up the stairs. Henry can't tell the crying of the beast from the wind. Outside, over the sea, the sky is a clot of clouds and darkness.

There is absolutely no moon.

CHAPTER 11

A t first Henry thinks it's the wind that wakes her, but it's the sound of Ndidi humming. When Henry cracks open her eyes, Ndidi is leaning over the edge of the bed, chin propped on one fist, and using her free hand to rock a basket on the floor beside her. Inside is a baby with its knuckle in its mouth, eyelids fluttering. Ndidi sees Henry sit up and lifts her chin, presses a finger to her lips.

When the baby is asleep, she goes on rocking the basket gently but whispers, "This one, she likes to sleep close. Especially after last night. I didn't want to sleep alone either."

"I saw that thing...the animal...in the forest when I was lost," Henry whispers back. "What *is* it?"

Ndidi shakes her head.

"I don't know. Neither does Wolfson, and if Wolfson doesn't know, then nobody does."

"What about Angie?"

"Everything Angie knows she tells Wolfson. I think she knows he's going to stay and stay. Like her."

"Is he okay after last night?"

"Hard to tell with him," Ndidi says. She stops rocking the basket and reaches down to stroke the baby's cheek, her touch as soft as a butterfly. She sighs. "I miss my cousins. One is little like this. How big they'll be by the time I get back..."

She trails off. Frowns a little. The room is starting to fill up with sunshine, but the baby's tiny chest goes on rising and falling slowly.

"No one knows where she came from?" Henry says, staring at the peaceful little face.

"She can't talk to tell us," Ndidi says sadly. "How do they figure out how to get home if they don't remember what home is?"

It would be so easy for Henry to tell her about her father. The embarrassment about going into the woods has even shrunk. But then Ndidi will ask, *How long was he gone?* and Henry will have to say a year. And Ndidi might say what Henry is already thinking: *How badly did he want to get home if it took him that long to leave This Place?*

113

"I can't believe I've been here this long," she says softly when Henry doesn't reply. "What if I'm here so long I don't remember home either?"

"Do you think that's part of why Wolfson stays?" Henry asks. "He was so little when he got here."

"I remember," Wolfson says. He stands in the doorway, another sleeping baby held against his shoulder. He's always appearing like this—Henry thinks he must have learned soft feet from his parents. "I remember enough to prefer it here. I'm glad you're awake," he says to Ndidi. "Angie is sending me to the junk man after breakfast. Want to help?"

Ndidi nods. "I'll take this little miss down to Javier." She looks over at Henry. "Want to come too?"

"Who's the junk man?"

"The man with all the junk," she teases. Whenever Ndidi teases, it's as if she's not sure about it. Henry remembers her report card this past year said, *Henry should practice speaking up.* This is Ndidi practicing.

Henry watches Wolfson, who sways to keep the baby asleep. He and Ndidi both seem good with babies—Henry doesn't think she's ever actually held one. None of her uncles or aunts have children—the one family reunion she remembers was small and awkward, and Henry was the only kid. She watched cartoons in Aunt Leslie's living room while the adults mumbled to one another.

"But what's going on with...the creature," Henry asks. "Did Angie say?"

"Henry says she saw it in the woods yesterday," Ndidi adds.

Wolfson tilts his head, thinking.

"So that *is* what you saw?" he says, raising an eyebrow. "I thought it might have been something from your world. But it was once you got to This Place?"

"I hadn't realized it yet, but yes. It was definitely the same thing. We don't have anything like that...at home."

"What if it got lost from some other world?" Ndidi says. "And it's stuck here too?"

"Then we should hurry up and get to the junk man," Wolfson says seriously.

"What if the beast is...out there?" Henry asks. "Waiting? Shouldn't we stay inside?"

"You'll never find your way out of This Place if you stay inside," Wolfson says. "Besides, thinking about it...the beast came at night, right? When it's dark. And I found you in the North Wood. That's where the forest is darkest. What if it can't be out in sunlight?"

"Sha, bats are nocturnal too," Ndidi says, looking doubtful. "And they have been out in the sun, acting odd."

"Yes, but the sunlight doesn't *hurt* them," Wolfson says. "Maybe it does hurt the beast? Henry, you came out of the woods and it didn't follow you, right?"

Henry nods in agreement. "And it's white like a cave fish. Like it's never even seen sunlight."

Wolfson nods. His smile is small but decisive.

"See? I think it will be all right. The junkyard isn't dark. We'll be back in plenty of time before the suns set."

Suns. Henry had forgotten there were two. The idea makes her shrink.

"It's okay," she says. "You guys go ahead."

Ndidi makes a face that wants to argue, to coax. But she nods. She carefully picks up the basket with the sleeping baby, then she and Wolfson are gone.

It's the first time Henry has been alone since she arrived here. She almost hopes this means that now she will shake herself and wake up. But nothing changes, and part of her wants to run after Ndidi and Wolfson, just to ask one more time if she's dreaming.

Sitting there in the quiet, Henry notices that she can smell her clothes. Whatever hole she fell through to end up here must have been real enough to have a stench. She strips the old clothes off and replaces them with the ones that appeared at the end of her bed. Pants and a shirt like everyone else, both dyed dark blue, little threads of silver spun in, like the backs of dolphins peeking through ocean. She wishes she knew where they came from—if not a dream, then what? Magic?

She balls up her worn clothes, chucks them into the basket.

116

Beside it is her father's pack, unbuckled and discarded when she came to bed. The sight of it plucks at her heart.

Inside, the map. Her father's handwriting. She digs her hand in.

In Quinvandel, she could have sworn the only thing in the pack was the map. Now her fingers run into something else— two somethings.

One hard and cold—a nail. She holds it up to the light. Rusty and old, almost like a railroad spike but much smaller. The other something feels almost feathery—a bit of beehive. She's seen pieces like this before when her mother cleaned out the garage, an ancient hive inside an old piece of gutter.

"Where did this come from?" she whispers to herself. But then there's the map, and she puts the nail and the hive back inside and gives the paper her attention.

She pulls it out carefully. Quinvandel, its dips and peaks in black ink. For the first time since she got lost, she feels that she might cry. First sad, then angry. What good was a map of Quinvandel when she was somewhere entirely different? She flings it off her lap. It doesn't go far, instead floating to the floor face down a foot away. The room looks blurry through her almost-tears, but then she sees the writing on the back of the paper. Red ink.

She lifts her head, curious. It must be the map's lines from the other side showing through.

But it's not. On the back of the map of Quinvandel is another map, this one written in red. She *knows* she didn't miss this in the forest. She had checked both sides, looking for her father's handwriting. And here it is, where it wasn't before. But the lines and shapes of the terrain aren't neat and printed like the map of Quinvandel. This is hand drawn, and the red ink is smudged in places. But she recognizes her father's handwriting, even if she can't read it all. Three words catch her eye:

The Pepper Sea

"This Place," she whispers.

The market
The junkyard

She holds the paper close to her face. Little drawings for each one. The certainty spreads through her. It's a map of This Place.

She was right. He had been here. And he'd been to the junkyard.

It had been sinking in slowly, but now the idea plummets through her. She shoves her feet into her sneakers, buckles her father's bag at her waist with the map inside, and then hurries out into the hall and down the stairs. Even if they've already left, perhaps she can catch up. She has a map, after all....

But when she rushes down into the dining room, Ndidi and Wolfson are sitting at one of the long tables, preparing to eat. Wolfson sees her, and he doesn't smile when he waves, but something about the way he moves his hand is friendly. Henry goes to join them.

"Changed your mind?" Ndidi says.

"Um, yes. Like you said...I probably can't leave here if I just stay in my room."

Henry isn't exactly sure why she lies. She's afraid that any second one of them will look at her pouch and say, *What's that you have in there?* She could tell them. But then she'd have to explain what she's going to do with the map, and Henry isn't sure yet. It's only a feeling: that she needs to walk where her father walked. It seems so simple in her mind. The map of This Place appeared once she crossed over, of that Henry is sure. And it means, she thinks, she has it for a reason.

"Not so bad, right?" Ndidi says, pointing at the blue clothes Henry now wears.

"They're so soft. You said Angie does the flowers—does she do the clothes too?"

"No," Wolfson says.

Henry thinks that at home people might think Wolfson is mean. His words have no cushion, and he uses so few of them.

119

That was what made Henry's mother tell her therapist she was quiet—so few words. Neither of them seemed to understand that talking too much felt like running out of air.

"So many things just show up," Ndidi goes on. "Like magic. But everything here has to be a little magic, okay? Look around o! There *has* to be a witch."

Wolfson shakes his head but doesn't speak. Henry looks around the dining hall. The window that was broken by the beast has been boarded up, but the other lets in daylight. Just outside, a horse and a tiger walk side by side in the morning sun. They move in an easy, relaxed way. They're strolling, she realizes. A horse and a tiger taking a morning stroll.

"What *is* This Place?" she breathes.

"Answered your own question," Ndidi says, and she gives the smile that looks like practice. For Ndidi it all feels like practice. This is the longest she has been away from her family, the longest she has gone without changing a diaper. She feels fidgety. Her hands and mind are usually so busy. She has nothing to think about but herself, and that feels strange.

Aside from the jagged hole where the window was broken, there are no other reminders of what happened the night before. All the glass has been swept up, and the children are smiling and milling around Javier, who is dropping food onto plates.

"Arepa!" one of the younger girls squeals. "Thank you, Javi!"

Henry realizes as she goes to get a plate that, as Ndidi requested egusi soup, someone has requested arepas as well. Everyone here is missing different parts of home, she thinks. What would she request if she asked Javier to make something? *Excuse me, Mr. Javi, can you make a black-bean burger like the ones in the green frozen package at home?*

"What are arepas?" she asks when she's sitting down between Ndidi and Wolfson. They've handed the babies off to Olga and an older boy, who have already eaten. Henry's plate has three golden disks on it, one by itself and the other two with what looks like beans and something like avocado.

"Not sure," Ndidi says, eating. She puts two of her disks together like a sandwich. "I think little Lilimar is from Venezuela."

"They're made from corn in her world," Wolfson says. "Not sure what Javier uses here to make it."

Henry takes a small bite, then a bigger one. It's good. She glances at Wolfson, who sits looking around the room but doesn't have a plate.

"Aren't you going to eat?" she asks around the big bite.

"Um...," he says. "No. I don't usually...um..."

"He doesn't eat," Ndidi supplies. "He doesn't really need to."

121

"What?"

"None of us actually do," he says. "Not here. Angie figured it out years ago."

Years ago is something Henry's grandmother would say. She thinks Wolfson kind of talks like a grandparent.

"Don't need to?" she says slowly. "Like…at all?"

"Our bodies don't need food here," Wolfson says, shrugging. "Whatever that means."

"Then why do I feel hungry?" Henry asks. Although suddenly she's not anymore.

"Memory," he says. She thinks he actually looks like a grandpa, too, sometimes—the way sadness gathers around the corners of his eyes. "Just like everything else, I guess."

Henry looks down at the arepa in her hand. It feels warm against her fingertips. The smell of it curls into her nostrils. She wants to ask if the food is even real, but she doesn't want to see that sadness on Wolfson's face again. And part of her doesn't want to know the answer at all. She takes another bite. Because even if she doesn't need to eat, she wants to.

Ndidi eats fast—her plate is almost empty. Henry chews faster. All around them are kids eating, and some of them look friendly, but some of them stare off into space. Some cry. It makes Henry feel like crying, too, but she has other plans now. She lays her hand against her father's pouch. She will walk where he walked, and following in his footsteps will lead her out of This Place. And when she gets back home, she decides, she will not be an earthworm anymore, but a butterfly.

The door of the hostel swings open, and in comes Angie, carrying a metal box. It's so big she clutches it to her chest, and she closes the door behind her with a kick of her foot. She comes straight to the table where Wolfson, Henry, and Ndidi sit.

"Still going to the junk man for me?" she says to Wolfson. He nods eagerly.

"Thank you." She beams at him, and he soaks it up like a plant. "You remember everything we need? Big planks of wood or sheets of metal. Nails, rope, duct tape. Things like that. I want to barricade the window that's broken, but I also want to reinforce the others in case that creature comes back."

"Do you think it will?" Henry asks.

Angie's eyes land on her.

"Henry," she says. "Are you settling in okay?"

Henry nods but returns to her question. "Do you think the beast will come back?"

After her father disappeared, Henry got very used to adults saying one thing and trying to use their face to hide the thing they really meant. She watches Angie do it now. Her forehead is working hard to stay smooth while she pretends not to be worried about the beast. But she is.

"I can't say for certain," Angie says. "I've never seen anything like it in This Place. But we'll figure it out. Everything will be okay."

"What if the witch sent the beast?" Ndidi says quickly.

"The witch?" Angie says, raising her eyebrows.

"I heard some adults talking about it a few days ago," Ndidi says, a little more softly now. Having Angie's full attention makes her shy. "About how things are changing in This Place—even before the beast showed up—and the witch is behind it."

"Things change in every world," Angie says. She loses the battle with her forehead. It wrinkles with worry. "I would guess that This Place is no exception. Doesn't mean there's a witch to blame!"

Angie manages a smile, and Wolfson reflects it back to her—it grows when her eyes return to his face.

"So," she says. "Wood. Metal. Nails. All that. You're okay going to see the junk man?"

"I'm not scared of Christopher," he answers.

Now Angie's face does something else. She almost winces.

"No, you don't have anything to fear from him. But be cautious anyway. He...well. He's him. You know!" Her smile looks propped up by a frown.

"What should I give him?" Wolfson asks. "You know he always wants something."

"Yes," Angie says quietly. "But never gets the thing he wants."

She hands Wolfson a tiny pouch.

"This should do," she says. Her face tries harder now to push away whatever worries are in her mind. Henry's mother has done the same thing a hundred times. "You've already asked the gray ladies to transport you?"

"Oh, right." Wolfson grins. He looks so different when he smiles at Angie. All the grandpa melts off him.

"What ladies? Transportation?" Ndidi asks, taking her last bite. "Does that mean we don't have to carry all that stuff back ourselves?"

"I'll introduce you," Wolfson says. He pushes back from the table, and so does Ndidi.

Adventure is out there, Henry reminds herself. She places her hand on her father's pack, just to make sure it's still there. Then she follows them, still chewing.

CHAPTER 12

The "ladies" Angie was referring to are a pair of donkeys. They go with Wolfson and the others to the junkyard, and they talk so much Henry finds it hard to focus on anything else.

I never thought I'd miss pulling a cart, Eunice says. *But this is nice. Just for a short while. To help out.*

I wouldn't have minded helping back at home if it wasn't for the bit, Eustace says. *I can't tolerate the bit.*

"What's the bit?" Wolfson asks, walking alongside Eunice.

A horrible thing humans put in our mouths, she says. *They do it to horses too. To steer.*

To control, Eustace emphasizes.

"Is the harness better?" Ndidi asks from the other side, next to Henry.

When it fits right, Eustace says. She turns her head toward Wolfson. *And it does, thank you.*

Wolfson nods back.

"Thanks for coming with us," he says. "We couldn't have done it without you."

We know, Eunice says, and even though her mouth doesn't smile, her eyes do, and something about her ears gives it away too.

The path winds back toward the town and its hostel, then winds forward away from the Pepper Sea. Forest in the far-off distance, and then what Henry thinks might be another town. As they get closer, the edges start to harden into shapes. But she's still looking all around. Everything green and open. Nowhere to hide if the beast comes back.

"Did you two, um, did you hear about what happened last night?" Henry asks Eunice and Eustace. She thinks it feels extremely strange to be talking to two donkeys, but the donkeys don't seem to share her discomfort. They're chatty and a little sarcastic, and if they notice Henry's hesitation, they ignore it.

How could we not? Eunice says. *All the screaming. Even over the rain. A terrible thing.*

We saw a bit of the creature, Eustace adds. *Running from the forest. A stumbling way of running. Not graceful at all.*

"Had you ever seen it before?" Ndidi says. "The beast?"

No, Eunice says. *Not here or home.*

Ah, here's the junkyard, Eustace says.

Henry sees it now, the shape she thought was a town. Now, closer, the junkyard reminds her of a shipwreck—the kind that has been sitting for so long that birds and animals have made a home of it. Even from a distance it looks dusty compared with all the untouched green of This Place. Her heart leaps in a way that makes her think of her father, and not only because the map says he has walked here.

Is this what he felt when he stumbled across that old moonshine rigging? Henry remembers that being his very first video that got over a million views. Joseph Lightfoot on *Good Morning America* and CNN, too, and, overnight, packages started arriving at the door to Henry's house, gifts from hiking-supply manufacturers and granola companies. As Henry and her group get closer to the junkyard, this feels like discovering. This is what her father must feel—striking out into the unknown and sensing the universe guiding him toward gold. Henry wishes she could pull the map out right then, see what else he might have marked around here. She tells herself she will as soon as she can get away by herself.

Closer still, she sees that comparing the junkyard to a shipwreck isn't wrong. Barnacles and seabirds making a home in wreckage isn't quite what this is, but it's close. Instead of seabirds flying toward wreckage, she thinks it's like the wreckage all flew toward itself, all the junk in This Place drawn together by a magnet she can't see.

There are cars—at least pieces of them—and broken windows, bicycles and small airplanes. Tables, chairs, big patio umbrellas. A few chimneys, all brick, as if they were lifted neatly off the roofs of houses. Mountains of shingles. A piano resting on the junkyard's roof. Small boats, mostly in pieces. Park benches. Birdbaths and limp hoses that might have been used to fill them. Tires and springs and pipes and wooden beams, and at the very top of the junkyard's front wall, a perfectly intact stained glass window, depicting a red-brown deer stretching its neck toward a clump of holly berries. It's all been arranged carefully, like a game of *Tetris* but with stuff instead of blocks. Henry decides it's not quite right to call it a junkyard. It's more like a junk *palace*.

For a minute, Henry isn't thinking about her father and his love of discovery—she's suddenly thinking about her mother. Missing her, hard, like someone suddenly yanked on a belt loop. Before, Henry's mother would sometimes take Henry to the antique shop while her father was out on adventures—that was where the two of them found his compass. Here, the turrets made of rusting bicycles make Henry think of that shop. It always smelled like furniture polish and basement, and after her father disappeared, sometimes her mother would go on a drive alone and come home smelling that way. Henry would imagine her walking through the tight aisles between ancient wardrobes, a maze more organized than her father's forests. Henry always felt like her mother was trying to get lost too.

"So what do we need?" Ndidi says, rubbing her hands together. "Lots of wood, right? Could probably yank down some of those doors up there..."

"Yes," Wolfson says. "But first we need to talk to Christopher."

Ndidi's hands fall to her sides. "Oh," she says.

"Christopher is the junk man?" Henry asks.

Yes, Eustace answers. *He built the junkyard.*

Henry takes in the turrets, the walls of stuff stacked and fitted together like brick and mortar.

"It must have taken forever," she breathes. "How long has he been here?"

"At least as long as me," says Wolfson, unhitching Eustace and Eunice. The two donkeys wander over to the shade of a tree that looks like the leg of an elephant. "Let's go. Try not to stare. And don't tell him where you're from. If he asks."

"Why—?" Henry starts, but he's already disappearing into the junkyard, and Ndidi only shrugs.

"I've never been inside either," she says. "Only heard rumors."

"What kind of rumors?" Henry whispers.

"The kind that are true," she answers.

Ndidi wavers at the door, unsure if she wants to go in at all, but Eunice and Eustace are watching the girls from the edges of their round brown eyes. Ndidi and Henry were born across the world from each other, but they have something in common: They are both very aware of when the adults in their lives don't want them around. The donkeys have this air—it's clear that they need to have a human-free conversation and Ndidi and Henry are in the way.

"Wolfson is in there alone," Ndidi says. This is something Ndidi is not comfortable with: leaving other children alone. Even if she is a child herself.

"Let's go," Henry says.

Inside is nothing like Henry expected.

It's beautiful and bright. Like that antique shop in Ripley, the ceiling is low and flat. But unlike the antique shop, it's transparent; made of what seems like overlapping sheets of glass. Not window glass, but something thick and almost plastic. An aquarium could have blown in on the wind, and the man they call Christopher salvaged some parts. Henry and Ndidi stand in an entrance hallway, surrounded by full shelves that turn a corner.

"Look," Ndidi says in a low voice, and Henry turns just in time to catch sight of a rainbow-colored bird disappearing into the space between two vases of marbles. The shelf itself seems to go on and on, filled with vases and fishbowls and upside-down motorcycle helmets, all filled with . . . stuff. Henry peers a little closer—she can see the bird's nest tucked in behind the glass jar of marbles.

"Good spot for a nest. It's so quiet in here."

Ndidi nods, and they both stand there for a moment, looking around. They're surprised, Henry thinks, by the way the junkyard isn't a pile of things people don't want but instead a museum of things people might need. Buttons and pennies and keys and rubber bands and paper clips and eyeglasses. The only sounds are birds singing and cooing and, somewhere, the rustling of wind through leaves.

Then the chime of a bell.

Ndidi and Henry follow the sound, leading them around the corner. They both gasp a little then—the hallway opens up, flat and wide. The ceiling is higher, and light pours in. For both girls it feels like a train platform, but with no trains. Instead of trains, there are the junkyard version of hills. And the closest one is a mound of yellow sweaters as tall as a garden shed.

None of them are folded, but all of them still feel neat—perhaps because the base of the mound seems to be on purpose. Not a single sleeve overlaps what is like an invisible line drawn around the marigold hill of wool and cashmere. And on the other side of it, fifty yards away, is Wolfson, standing at a long wooden desk, bumpy like it was carved out of driftwood. His hand hovers over a tiny bell like the one on the counter of the greasy old diner Henry went to for bacon and eggs sometimes with her mother. And her father. Before.

The chime in the junkyard almost sounds like one of the birds. Henry wonders how often people in This Place come here, if that bell is rung a lot or if the rumors about Christopher keep this room empty. Her heart beats faster now that Wolfson has rung the bell. Ndidi didn't tell Henry what the rumors actually are, so now her brain creates its own ideas about Christopher. Maybe he's a pirate. A king of thieves.

As it turns out, he's a giant.

CHAPTER 13

Sha, have you ever...?" Ndidi whispers when Christopher steps out from the curtains that hang behind the desk. Henry barely recognizes him as a person at first. Her mind says: *Truck. Building. Construction machine.* Because Christopher is too big to be a person. Henry's uncle Cecil loves sports and has always shouted at the TV for everything from football to hockey, but Henry thinks if Christopher were on the field, the athletes would all look like children. He's as tall as a car stood up on its bumper, and almost as wide.

"Hi, Christopher," says Wolfson. "Angie sent me."

"Wolfson," Christopher says. Henry expected the voice of a mountain, but instead it's the voice of a regular-sized boulder. Deep and craggy, but the ground doesn't shake and the ceiling doesn't cave in. Christopher sounds like a normal human, Henry thinks, and not like a pirate or a villain at all. She and Ndidi exchange a look and move closer, passing the mountain of yellow sweaters. On the other side of it the girls find other mounds of clothes: a red hill of jackets. A peak of jeans, all shades of blue. Christopher doesn't even seem to notice the two of them.

"If Angie sent you," he goes on, still looking at Wolfson, "then she didn't send you empty-handed."

"No, she didn't," Wolfson says. He opens the tiny pouch that Angie provided while Henry studies Christopher. He's white, with long hair past his shoulders that's tied away from his face with a strip of cloth. His face has the tight tan skin of a sunburn that doesn't turn red anymore, eyes a watery blue, almost muddy. They flick up to look at Henry and Ndidi but barely rest before going back to Wolfson, who is pulling his fingers out of the pouch.

"This is what she sent?" Christopher mutters when he sees what's in Wolfson's hand. "Your boss is a cruel one."

"Angie's not my boss," Wolfson says firmly.

Ndidi and Henry move slowly closer, curious. Whatever it is, it's tiny in Christopher's tray-sized hand.

"Seeds?" Ndidi says, surprised.

Henry is surprised too—she'd expected gold or some kind of money This Place uses that she just hasn't seen yet. But when she looks closer, she sees they're not even seeds.

"Cherry pits," Henry says out loud.

Christopher's palm closes over them quickly.

"Go pick what you need," he says. "Wood only."

"And nails?" Wolfson ventures.

"Fine."

Wolfson gestures with his head for Henry and Ndidi to follow, and they do, moving around the many small mountains back toward where they came in. When Henry glances at Christopher, he seems smaller. No, she thinks: He definitely is smaller. His head was grazing the plants that hang from the glass ceiling when they walked in. Now the plants hang over him like streamers at a birthday party. Christopher still stares down at the cherry pits in his hand when Wolfson nudges Henry.

"I'll go get Eunice and Eustace," he says, and points. "You two walk that way until you see wood. It's a whole section. There's another entrance down there where I'll meet you so we don't have to walk so far with heavy stuff."

Henry and Ndidi wander down the long aisle Wolfson pointed toward, checking out all the junk. Henry still wonders who named this a junkyard, because the more she sees of it, the more it reminds her of a museum. Watches and cuff links and enamel pins and spools of cords. The girls keep walking until the objects on the shelves gradually begin to get bigger and no longer fit in jars. Oars and doors like the

136

ones that were used to make the building itself—they're all arranged in collections of leaning stacks. Like the sweaters, they're color coded. Light wood, dark wood, red-painted.

There are blue-painted ones, too, and a wave of homesickness swoops down on Henry like a barn owl. At home she would turn the handle of a blue door and find herself in her living room. Here, she wouldn't find herself at all. She would just find more blue doors, all of them chipped and battered. She wonders for the first time how they all got here.

Ndidi must have been thinking the same thing, because she runs her fingertips along some of the door panels.

"When I was little," she says, "there was a storm so strong it picked up my uncle's car. They never found it. I wonder if I would find it here if I looked hard enough."

"Maybe so," Henry says. But she's not thinking about cars or doors. She's thinking about her father. The junkyard is on the map in her pack, and that must mean he came here and met Christopher. Not telling Ndidi and Wolfson about her father means she can't ask Christopher about him in front of them. But she can't think of a good enough reason to go back and talk to the giant, and she's not sure if she'd want to be alone with him anyway.

"Found some good stuff." Wolfson pops out from a gap in the shelves. "We'll have everything we need."

They round a corner into a short corridor. Sunlight pours

in from outside, through a door made of driftwood that's been swung open. Outside, Eustace and Eunice stand with the wagon, faces turned toward each other, chatting silently.

Wolfson *has* found some good stuff. Driftwood and windowpanes without the glass. The driftwood comes in all shapes and sizes, which the three of them agree will be perfect for blocking the hole the beast left. They find long slats to go across the unbroken windows. They drag pieces out to the wagon one at a time and haul them up into it. It's getting full when Ndidi pauses.

"He said we could take nails too?"

Wolfson nods.

"Where are they?" She looks around.

"Metal section," Wolfson says, tossing a piece of driftwood into the wagon. "I should've thought of that. It's back closer to Christopher's desk."

"Who's going to get them?" Ndidi asks nervously. "I don't want to be around that man o."

Henry sees her opportunity and answers quickly.

"I'll do it. I don't mind."

Wolfson looks up at the sky. The two suns have shifted lower—they've been working for a while.

"Maybe go now while we finish loading," he says, "so we can leave as soon as you're back."

Henry tries not to look too guilty when she tosses a piece

138

of driftwood into the wagon. If she seems too eager to go, they might wonder why. All she wants is to ask Christopher if he's ever met her father. She wants to look at the map.

"Be right back," she tells them, and hurries inside.

Once Wolfson and Ndidi are out of sight, her feet slow. It's only when Henry is alone that This Place starts to feel scary.

"Dad wouldn't be scared," she whispers. "Dad wouldn't be scared."

She pulls the map from her pocket. Unfolded, the veins of red ink sprawl out. There's the Pepper Sea. There's the junkyard, the very same one she's standing in now. There are the mountains, the forests. There's even the mouth of a cave in an area of the map that might be near Wolfson's parents' place. Not everything is labeled, like the cave. Some things have only little pictures. One, a tall tree. Another, something that could be either a lake or a pond. Small with little sketches of water waves drawn in. There, at the top of the map, an X. Whatever her father had used to write with, he had gone over the X a few times.

"X marks the spot," she murmurs.

But the spot of what? It could just as easily be a mark to get the ink flowing. The map gives her more questions than answers. The only thing that's sure is he must have seen these places—her father wouldn't have drawn them on otherwise. He always had to see everything himself. He and his cameraman, Jemmy, fought about it, she remembers—Jemmy telling her father he'd seen a cave and Dad not being satisfied until he had seen it himself. This included things that were off-limits. Trails that were closed, monuments roped off. Henry's father didn't care about rules. He wanted to touch everything.

Henry looks up from the map, at the long hall she now stands in. She's still afraid of Christopher. He seems to have strict rules about what happens in his kingdom of junk, and she thinks he didn't exactly seem like the talkative type for questions.

"Dad wouldn't be scared," she whispers again.

Then something catches Henry's eye in another of the short corridors that connect to the main aisle. It's not the soft green glimmer that comes down from the plants on the rooftop. It's sharper and bright. Metal. She leans into the mouth of the corridor, looking for the nails she said she'd go get. Maybe she will just grab some and scratch the plan of talking to Christopher at all. She can ask someone else if her father sounds familiar. Angie, maybe.

But once she's in the corridor, nails aren't what keeps her attention. There are tons of jars full of various random things—belt buckles and dog collars, bowls and bowls of watches. And beside the watches are more bowls, these filled with compasses, some with covers and some shining and open, some of their markings simple and others ornate.

Resting at the edge of one of the bowls is one she recognizes.

Silver and scuffed, with a gold face and distinctive letters for north, south, east, and west. In the center, a swooping swallow. It's strange seeing it here in this building that smells like an antique store because the first time Henry saw it had been in an actual antique store. Fourth grade, and two weeks before Father's Day. Her mother dragging her along to choose a gift in the aisles of ancient stuff she loved picking through. The two of them found the compass on a shelf between an old cigarette lighter and a money clip, and they knew it was the perfect gift right away. *We'll just make it a little more personal before we give it to him*, her mother said.

Henry's hands shake a little as she reaches for the compass—she knows it's his before she even picks it up and checks for the engraving on the back. But when she see the words etched in metal, her heart feels like a broken elevator anyway.

Home is the best North Star.

She's glad Ndidi and Wolfson aren't here to see her eyes well up. Henry has never been much of a crier. But this is her father's compass. The one she gave him. And it's here.

"That's not a nail," says a voice from above.

Christopher is a giant again, tree-ish in the way he blocks out so much light.

141

"This is my dad's," she says, forgetting all the ways she'd come up with to ask him if he'd ever met a Joe Lightfoot with blue eyes and a beard. She doesn't need to ask. The proof is in her hand.

"Was it?" Christopher asks.

"Why do you have this?"

"I'm the junk man." He shrugs. He looks even bigger somehow.

"This isn't junk."

"I would argue that nothing here is. One man's trash is another man's treasure."

"This is my dad's," she repeats. "It wasn't trash to him either."

"Perhaps he lost it," Christopher says. He stares at Henry the way animals at the zoo do. Like there's something between them other than air.

"Is that where all this stuff comes from?" she asks, pointing all around them, at the watches and buttons and the swarms of wind chimes she hadn't even noticed until now. "It's lost?"

"You'd do better to ask Angie," he says, and now he looks smaller than before. Henry thinks it's like moving a magnifying glass close to and then far in front of her eye. Still, she can never quite catch him changing—like it happens when she blinks.

She swallows and try to think like her father.

"I thought *you* were the junk man," she says.

"I am," he says. "But that doesn't mean I know where it all comes from. We barely know how *we* get here, let alone what makes *things* show up. Some of it disappears. Some of it doesn't. Things people take with them, what they leave behind."

"My dad wouldn't have left this behind," she says, and hopes she sounds sure.

He shrugs, then points over her shoulder.

"Nails are there," he says. "If you want a hammer, you'll need something else to trade."

"Like cherry pits?" she asks before he can walk away. He doesn't seem so scary now. Maybe because he's not as giant as he was before.

"Special accommodation," he answers. "I usually trade for more than seeds."

"Did my dad trade you this compass for something?"

"I trade with a lot of people," he says, and now he's a giant again, turning his back.

"Wait," she cries, and goes after him. "Aren't you even going to try to remember? I can tell you what he looks like. His name is Joseph Lightfoot and—"

"This Place doesn't work the way our world worked, kid," he says, still moving away down the main aisle. "Time doesn't make sense, especially lately. What feels like two days at home may be two years here. Or two seconds. What *lost* means is different to everyone, you see? If your dad was here, it could feel like a decade to me. Besides, I remember things, not people. That's part of why I'm in This Place."

And just like that, he's the smallest she's seen him. He's barely taller than Henry. She reaches out and catches a bit of his shirt before he can go away. He turns on her, surprised, then he looks down at himself, the distance to the floor, and sighs.

"What, kid?"

She wants to hide. But she reminds herself she's walking in her father's footprints now.

"You may not remember this compass," she says, holding it up. "But I do. Me and my mom got it for my dad on Father's Day. It was his. And he wouldn't have left it behind. It was..." She remembers her father's face, saying thank you. *This is precious to me.* "It was precious to him. He just got back home yesterday. Or whatever yesterday is at home."

She stops, doubt sinking in. She's been rushing to figure out a way to get home, but what if it's already been a year? When she thinks of her mother, again going through what she went through when her father was missing, it makes it hard to swallow.

"*Precious* means different things here too," Christopher says, taking the compass from Henry's hand and staring at it. "This Place will show you what you think you really need,

144

wrong or right. If he went home and left this here, that's his business."

"Give it back to me, then," she says. "I'll take it home… when I get out of here."

"You'll have to trade," he says. Now she has to crane her head back to look him in the face. "Nothing free in This Place."

"But it's my dad's," she cries. "That engraving on the back…"

"It's junk now," he says, pulling away and moving down the hall in giant steps. "You want to bring me something to trade for, I'll consider it."

Then she remembers. She rests her hand on her chest, on top of where the necklace her father brought her hangs.

"You said you don't remember people," she calls after him. "But you remember things. Do you remember trading for a necklace? It's all he came home with. Did he get it from you?"

Christopher stops in the middle of the aisle, not looking back.

"What kind of necklace?" he says a moment later.

"Silver. Round like a river stone. A fine chain."

"Do you have it with you?"

She thinks of what Ndidi said—the rumors about Christopher. Maybe he had *taken* her father's compass, not traded. She doesn't want him to take her necklace too.

"No—"

He shakes his head abruptly, then keeps walking.

"Junk," he calls over his shoulder, his voice booming in the aisle. "Come back when you have something worth trading for."

He disappears around a corner, swallowed by the shelves packed with objects. Henry's hands feel cold where they'd been clutching the compass, and her eyes feel like they could cry again. Seeing the compass here fills her mouth with the taste just after vomit. Sour and burny, not even wanting water, because that would mean swallowing. It's not Christopher keeping the compass that makes her feel this way. It's what he said. What if her father *did* leave the compass on purpose? The idea that what is precious to Henry isn't precious to him makes her feel sad and sick at the same time.

But there's nothing left to do or say. She turns and walks back to where she left Ndidi and Wolfson.

Her father had been here. Henry was right. And at first it made her feel better, because no, he hadn't been off on a grand adventure without her and her mother. He'd been stuck here, trying to find a way home. But why he would he trade the compass?

Whenever Henry did the thing her counselor told Henry not to do—imagine scenarios of her father, things he might have done before he died out there, when she thought he was dead—she imagined him crouched in a cave with no light, using his fingers to trace the words engraved on the back of the compass. Except now it seems like her father traded away the thing that was supposed to keep him going. So what kept him going instead?

She doesn't even notice when her feet have carried her back to where Ndidi and Wolfson are lifting one last big plank of driftwood until Ndidi sees her and brightens.

"We thought Christopher might have eaten you o! Are you okay?"

Henry looks up, barely hearing.

"Huh? Oh. No. I'm fine."

She follows them out to the wagon, and only after watching them struggle to load the wood for a minute does she realize she should help.

"Sorry," she grumbles, and the three of them wrestle it up onto the back.

"It's too long to let us close the back of the wagon," Wolfson says. "But we won't go too fast. Eustace, Eunice, is this okay? Is it too heavy?"

Too heavy, Eunice scoffs, twitching her ears, and says nothing else. Henry thinks that means it's okay.

"Where are the nails?" Ndidi says, turning her eyes back to Henry.

Henry only stares blankly until it sinks in.

"Crap," she cries, and slaps her palms against her eyes.

"What, no nails? Abeg, where were you all this time if not getting nails?"

"I was talking to Christopher, okay?" Henry bursts out. "I...I found something in the metal section and then we..."

"But...but..." Ndidi's face looks like it's fighting with itself. When she speaks again, it's the wobbly tone of a child who has been told not to cry. "But we don't have what we need. And we need to hurry to get back before dark!"

Henry's face burns. So many little things piling and piling. Big things too. A year without her father, Uncle Cecil saying what he said, This Place, the compass.

"There's other things happening than a broken window," Henry cries. "I've got things on my mind. I'm sorry I forgot the stupid nails!"

"Things on your mind?" Ndidi says. "Yes, you are the only one with things on your mind, surely. In This Place that does not exist where we are unsure if we will ever see family or eat rice again, you are the only one with things on your mind. Your mind is full full. I'm so sorry o!"

Ndidi clasps her hands when she finishes speaking, staring down at them. And for a moment, she seems to flicker in the dimming sun. Wolfson looks as surprised as she does, as if neither of them can believe she said so much. But when he looks back over at Henry, she can tell he agrees with Ndidi.

The weight of it makes her turn her back on them both. She marches past the wagons and the donkeys, down the path. And after a few steps, she begins to jog. Then the jog becomes a run. She wants the junkyard behind her. She wants Christopher and the compass and everything else behind her. And she doesn't want anyone to see her cry.

"Henry, don't!" Ndidi calls.

But she ignores Ndidi, and Wolfson, too, when he shouts. If she turns and speaks again, everything inside her will come pouring out, and she doesn't think there's enough space—even in the junkyard—for all the mess in her heart. Wolfson is yelling, "Just let me give you…" But Henry doesn't want anything he has. She doesn't want anything This Place has to offer.

CHAPTER 14

Henry thought she couldn't get lost when she was already in the land of the lost.

She was wrong.

She finds herself in a forest where the trees are all white and thin and reach up to the sky like desperate swords. The leaves are pale green, as if their chlorophyll is stuck in the throats of the trunks. And then there's the silence. It reminds her of one winter at her grandmother's house out in the country. They all had to stay through the weekend because the snow was too deep. They stepped out onto the back porch, and to Henry it felt like the whole world was on mute. Like the snow was a layer between awake and asleep. This forest feels like that.

Every step she takes should make some kind of sound—pale green leaves carpet the ground. But they seem too limp and lifeless to crackle. And besides, Henry is used to walking softly. At home, in the first month after her father disappeared, her mom would whirl around in her chair whenever Henry walked into the room, like she expected her daughter to be him, sneaking in to surprise her. Eventually Henry learned to move quietly—she couldn't take the look of disappointment that settled in her mother's eyes over and over again. So Henry makes her way through this pale forest like a ghost.

And like a ghost, she ends up in the dark. Too fast. Time doesn't make sense in This Place, and Henry knew that, but she'd left the junkyard anyway. Her father had been like that—blowing off steam on a quick hike. Except he knew not to go anywhere without his compass. A compass that now sits in Christopher's kingdom of junk.

Moonlight breaks through the trees. It's sharp and white in the thick black. But when Henry tilts her head up to see the moon itself, the sky looks flat and empty. Part of it looks even blacker, where the moon might have been.

What she thought was moonlight disappears. Then reappears, this time farther to her left. It can't be moonlight. Too low. And moonlight doesn't rattle the tree branches.

Her spine goes as rigid as one of the white trees.

"Oh no." It's barely a whisper, but it still sounds too loud, and she claps a hand over her mouth. *Beasts.*

Henry clutches the necklace her father gave her. When she was small she would call him into her room and complain about the shadows. The streetlight outside their old house turned everything in her room into a monster. Every night he would show her what each thing really was—lamp, teddy bear, hanging coat. But this isn't her bedroom, and the shadows aren't harmless. Henry can't tell if the sound she hears is the wind through the trees or the parting of those glowing teeth.

She turns and runs.

Directionless. Everything looks the same in the dark, and without the moon she doesn't know how she can see at all. The white trees themselves seem to let off a small light—almost like glowworms on the walls of caves. Is this whole place the cave that swallowed her father? Will it now swallow Henry? Or will the beasts do it first?

She zigzags through the trees. Even in daylight, nothing would be familiar. But behind her she hears something crashing through the underbrush, and now she's not looking for familiar—she's just looking for a place to hide. The necklace thumps against her chest so hard that she grips it tightly in one hand and runs as fast as she can.

There's more than one of them. She can hear them all around. She has never felt her lungs the way she does now.

She suddenly thinks of Ibtihaj at home—how on Field Day in fourth grade she had a broken foot and Henry had to run a three-legged race with someone other than her. Henry doesn't remember whom. All she remembers is Ibtihaj on the sidelines in her purple cast, her voice cutting through everyone else's, yelling, *Go, go, go!*

There should be an end to the forest, but there isn't. It goes on and on. Henry's running out of breath, and underneath she feels a burst of outrageous hope, that maybe she'll fall through another cave, end up at her own front door. Every step that lands on solid ground instead is like a punch through her heart.

But the trees are certainly glowing—the forest breaks ahead, and there it's dark. It reminds her of the fields of tobacco plants near Uncle Cecil's—vegetation low and thick. A good place to hide. She plunges forward, then throws herself down to the ground, crawling low with her back dropped to keep from rustling the leaves.

She breathes through her nose instead of panting, even though it feels like sucking air through a straw. Too much breath. Too much fear. She can hear the beasts. She's sure it's them now. She recognizes the snuffling, the careful sound of them placing their paws. She gets a glimpse. They move like water. Or like they should be flying, she thinks. They're so quiet now. They're smelling for her.

And they're getting closer.

Henry shifts her weight onto her hands, carefully rotating her body so she doesn't have her back to them. She crawls backward under the heavy branches of the plants—tiny plants that look like full-grown trees, but waist high. She creeps under their miniature canopy, praying she doesn't step on a twig. The light that cracks through the leaves isn't moonlight. The moon is gone, she remembers. It's the glow of the white beasts. By the time Henry realizes she should've kept running, they're too close. She can smell them now—their breath carries a scent like melting snow.

She leaps upright out of the field of tiny trees and she must surprise them—the one in front rears back, teeth bared. Of all the tiny things Henry found in her father's pack, one of them wasn't bear spray. Would it even work on creatures like them? She waves her arms, wondering if she's handling the wild animals the way her father taught her. All the dos and don'ts run together in her mind, and now it's time to run again, before they leap.

Someone is shouting.

It's not Henry. Someone else. Her heart screams *Ibtihaj*, but it's not her either. A woman appears beside Henry, white and thin, carrying a torch. She waves it toward the beasts and shouts in a muffled voice. The beasts flinch away. But even as they do, their eyes are fixed on Henry. She feels their eyes practically burn a hole in her chest. She clutches the necklace her father gave her—the white stone fills her palm. The beasts seem to salivate.

The woman reaches out and takes a firm hold of Henry's arm, pulling her along as they both walk backward. One beast moves to follow, and the woman waves the torch again. Her voice sounds like she's speaking underwater, a current carrying off the words.

The beasts keep their distance, and the woman with Henry backs away and away. Henry feels dizzy, like the world is spinning and standing still at the same time. The miniature trees around her brushed her hips before, but now meet her rib cage, and now her neck. Henry thinks she must be falling slowly, so slowly it's like floating. The beasts get bigger but farther at the same time. By the time the dizzy feeling passes, the beasts are gone—nothing but sky far above trees whose tops are too high to see.

Henry stumbles and doesn't think she'll actually fall, but she does. She lands hard, then stares up at the woman with the torch, and the woman stares back down at Henry where she sits on blanketed pine needles. The woman's mouth moves, but all Henry hears is the ocean sound.

They both realize it at the same time.

The woman reaches into the pouch of her sweatshirt, which is woven with multicolored thread, many scraps sewn together. It has a hood and a pouch sewn on like a kanga-roo's. When she withdraws her hand, she's holding between two fingers a red berry just like the one Wolfson gave Henry. Makab.

Henry takes it without questioning and places it on her tongue. Its slightly sour juice spreads through her mouth before she swallows it away. Nothing else changes. But when the woman with the torch opens her mouth, Henry can understand her this time:

"You must be Joseph's child."

CHAPTER 15

The woman's name is Emma, and she lives in a part of This Place that sees no visitors.

"I wonder if anyone thinks I've found my way," she says as she makes a sandwich. "Because they haven't seen me for so long. Maybe most of them never noticed me at all."

She'd given Henry a blanket when they'd arrived in her house, thinking she was cold. But Henry is still shaking, even with it wrapped around her. *Adrenaline*, she hears in her father's voice. He'd made a video that went viral after he met a grizzly face-to-face on one of his trips. *I shook for three hours after this*, he said into the camera. *Humans aren't used to the feeling of being hunted anymore.*

Henry remembers that being what he called "a tough

day on the internet." For the first time his comment section wasn't full of worshippers. Instead, people said things like, "You think this because you're a white man." Henry and Ibtihaj read the comments on the computer screen at her house. "They're not exactly wrong," her best friend said. Secretly, Henry didn't think the commenters were wrong either. But she didn't tell her dad that.

"How did you know my dad?" she asks Emma. Emma, who knew her father's name. Emma mutters a lot. Drifts around the kitchen in constant motion, grabbing a spoon in one rotation and a plate the next. The sandwich slowly comes together.

"Sunflower butter," she says. "I think. Jelly is strawberry. Or close enough."

The plate ends up on the table in front of Henry. She thinks of what she learned about not eating in This Place. Not needing it. Henry stares down at the sandwich, wondering if she should refuse it. She's here, isn't she? Maybe she should get used to not eating. But she doesn't want to get used to it. And the way Emma has cut the sandwich into two triangles makes Henry think of her mother.

"How did you know my dad?" Henry asks again, chewing.

"How else?" Emma says. She has lank hair the color of wheat that almost reaches her waist, and when she leans against the kitchen counter she takes her hair in her fists and pulls it over the front of her body. "This Place."

"How long have you been here?"

"Longer than you," she says. "Since you're asking that question. Long enough to know that time doesn't make sense here."

Emma has to be Henry's mother's age, but something about the way she talks reminds Henry of kids at school.

"I like it here," Emma says. "Especially in the Small Part."

"Don't you get lonely?"

Emma frowns a little at that. She doesn't answer.

"How did you find the Small Part?" Henry tries. Now that she's eating, her body has stopped shaking so much. She lets the blanket fall off her shoulders. Even if the food isn't real, or however it works, the feeling of eating does something to her brain. Pieces of a collage coming together to make a full picture. The plants and the trees and the falling away from the beasts. Henry thinks of the trees that were at her ankles one moment and at her neck the next. She remembers Christopher, the way he was first a giant, and then barely taller than her, all in a split second. "Did we shrink?"

"Either that or everything else gets bigger," Emma says. She lets her hair go, and it swings slowly down to her sides. "I don't know. Who cares."

"Don't you want to know how it works?"

"What would it change? Nothing. Does it matter if this kitchen is actually tiny or if the world outside it is big? I'm small either way."

Henry looks around the woman's house. The kitchen is practically all of it. In the corners are crates and bags. A large tank that looks like the kind they have at fairs, full of helium. On one side of the room is a bunk bed. The bottom bunk is made neatly—tight like a military bed. The top bunk is a big pile of covers.

"You're alone here?" Henry asks.

"I'm alone everywhere. What were the beasts?"

Henry stops chewing, surprised. "You're asking me?"

"Yes. You brought them."

"I didn't *bring* them. They were chasing me."

"Same difference."

She really is like talking to another kid, Henry thinks.

"Okay, well, you seemed to know how to handle them," Henry says. "With the torch and stuff."

"Well, I've dealt with them before."

"You have? Then why are you asking me what they are? Don't you know?"

"I wouldn't ask if I *knew*!" she cries.

Henry puts the sandwich down. If it were a kid at school, she would walk away and go sit next to Ibtihaj. Emma makes

160

her want to cry the same way Melinda sometimes did. But in the pack at Henry's waist is her father's map. She takes a deep breath.

"Please tell me about my dad."

"Joseph," Emma says. "He was here a long time ago. Or maybe not. Who knows."

"Did you talk to him?"

"Joseph talked to everyone," Emma says. "He found me when I was in the forest near the junkyard. I told him about the Small Part. He wouldn't let it rest until I brought him here. Wasn't sure I could, actually. But it worked out. He wanted to map it all."

Henry opens the pack and reaches inside.

"This map?" she says, holding it up.

Emma pushes off the counter and comes near. She stares at the map for a long time, studying every inch. Henry can hear her father's voice in her head: *Today, sweetheart.* She almost says it, just to hear if her voice can sound like his. But then Emma sniffs.

"That's the one."

"Can you show me where I am?" Henry says, pointing at the map. "I got turned around when I was running from the beasts."

"Oh, I said he *wanted* to map it all, not that he *did*. Where we are isn't on that map. I told him it wouldn't stick."

"Wouldn't stick?"

"This is the Small Part. It doesn't stay put. He tried a few times and then gave up. On to the next part of his adventure."

Henry's heart sinks. "Do you know where he went after this?"

"The junkyard, if I recall," she says, frowning. "I told him he'd find it interesting. He was looking for equipment, and I told him that if it was to be had, then Christopher would have it."

She finishes on a bitter note. Her scowl says there's nothing more to be shared.

"Oh," Henry says. There was a hot-air balloon in her chest, and now it slowly sinks back to earth.

Emma seems to notice.

"What's the matter?" she says, eyeing her.

"Nothing..." It seems silly to say out loud now. "I just...I had this idea...."

"What idea?"

"To...follow him."

"He's still here?"

"No, no...he...he's home."

"Ah, I see. You think if you retrace his steps, you'll find your way out, is that it? That's what you do with a lost thing, right? You misplace a scarf, you retrace your steps until you and it are reunited."

162

Henry could tell her that's part of it. She could tell her that, yes, following in his steps is the start. But Henry is also talking about when she gets back, when she and her father are both found again. She can almost feel the shape of all the things she wants to say: that when her father was gone, she felt left behind. And that's a feeling she'd like to get rid of when she leaves This Place.

"I think I still have something of his," Emma says suddenly. "Stay there."

Henry sits straight up.

"Something of my dad's? What is it?"

Emma waves Henry off in answer and digs around in a drawer in her kitchen, muttering to herself and riffling through objects.

"No, that was the woman from Iceland. Oh, I remember this. He was so kind. Oh, a tennis ball. Silly thing to have come to This Place with. Oh, her. I think she was from Thailand. Here it is," she says triumphantly.

But when she turns around, Henry sees that all she has is a wad of paper.

"What...what is that?"

"I don't know," Emma says. "But it was his."

Henry slowly takes the paper from her. She feels like crying. She doesn't know what she hoped Emma had, but she wasn't expecting...trash.

"Uncrumple it," Emma says around the bite of Henry's sandwich she's just taken.

She does, carefully. And she finds her father's handwriting.

"Good, right?" Emma says, chewing.

I'd like a whole collection when I leave This Place. Little pieces from every part.

Henry stares at the scrap of paper in her hand. It's small—ripped from his tiny journal, she thinks. The yellow one he wrote in with the bowling-alley pencil.

"Collecting," she says. Her heart sinks lower. Nothing about Henry, nothing about the compass and how difficult it might have been to part with. Just more collecting. Things for his basement shelves.

"Little things," Emma says, thinking Henry is asking a question. "He took a nail I intended to put in my roof. Didn't even ask. Gotta say, your father, Joseph, wasn't the most well liked while he was here."

Henry hears *nail*.

"Did you say a nail?" she asks.

"Yes. Said it looked antique. Maybe it was. Who knows how old things are here."

Henry unzips the small pack and reaches inside.

"This?" she says, holding up the nail. It's blunted with age, a little mossy.

Emma studies the nail without touching it. By the look in her eyes, Henry can see that Emma has had things taken before. But maybe she's never had something returned. It's such a small thing, a nail. But joy passes over her face before it settles back into a mask of petulance.

"Come outside," Emma says. She tosses the sandwich onto the plate and stands up. "You can hold the ladder."

"Huh? Ladder?"

"Yes. So I don't fall."

"Now? Isn't it too dark?"

"You'll be gone before morning. I have lamps."

Henry carefully tucks her father's note into the pouch along with the map, then follows Emma outside, carrying the nail.

"Did he give you that note?" Henry asks.

"No, fell out of his pack."

"And you kept it?"

"Sure. Nothing is an accident."

For a second, the sight of Emma seems to flicker. She pauses, glancing down. When nothing more happens, she continues down the porch steps.

"It's a good ladder," she says. "I brought it all the way from

Christopher's. Without the benefit of a cart. The donkeys don't like me much. Wouldn't even take pay. Ridiculous to pay a donkey anyway."

Henry bites her tongue. She's exchanged only a few words with the ladies, but she knows if she called it ridiculous in front of them, they would have some things to say.

"One of the trees fell some time ago, you see?" Emma says. "I've been meaning to fix the weather vane. See it leaning? Can't get up there without someone to hold the ladder."

Before they went into the house, Emma had placed the torch she used to scare off the beasts into a sconce. Now she takes it up again and lights what looks like a rope hanging from the edge of the house.

"Wait," Henry gasps, but the fire is already racing hungrily along the woven path, ripping toward the house. Henry steps back, hand over her mouth.

"Not real fire," Emma says. "Not real food, not real fire. Light is just light here, and nothing else."

Henry doesn't understand, but Emma's right—the fire doesn't spread the way real fire would. The heat of it sticks to the rope, as if it were coated in glowing paint. It illuminates the outside of Emma's little house, roof slanted and chimney cold.

Then there's the ladder. It leans against the house like it's tired after a run—crooked and a little bowed in the middle.

166

Henry doesn't exactly think it looks safe. She saw many ladders in Christopher's kingdom and wonders how long ago Emma went and got this one.

"You stand here," Emma says, pointing. "And hold it. Both hands."

Henry braces herself next to the ladder and grips both sides. Whenever her mother would get nervous about her father going off on an adventure, he would say, "I'm more likely to fall off a ladder. Household falls are what you should worry about!" Every therapy session since he'd disappeared, Henry and her counselor talked about things like that. Letting go of things like that. How people can say things won't happen, but saying it doesn't make those words magic. That has been the hardest part. The thing he always said wouldn't happen, did.

But her father came back, Henry reminds herself.

"Did my dad stay long?" she asks Emma.

Emma takes the old nail from Henry's hand without answering. When she reaches the ladder, she climbs so slowly that Henry wonders if, despite having a face as young as her mother's, Emma is closer to eighty years old. She never moves a hand or a foot at the same time. One, then one, then one.

Emma eventually answers.

"He was here for a bit," she says. "Most people wig out. He didn't. He caught on fast."

"That's my dad," Henry says.

"You can tell from the note that he liked it here," she says. "A loner, but a happy one. Exploring, walking around, touching things."

Why does the idea of him being happy make Henry so sad? It fills her with guilt. Emma doesn't notice.

"I talked to everyone, too, my first time," Emma mutters. She's going on climbing slowly. One foot, one rung. "Wrote down a list of all the people I met while I was here. But when I got back, it was all gibberish. Chicken scratch. You don't take anyone's story from here but your own."

Henry lets the words sink in.

"Wait, the first time? Does that mean… Wait, you're the person who was here twice! Is that you?"

Emma pauses her turtle-slow climb to peer back down at Henry.

"Who told you that?"

"I mean, you just did."

"No, before just now."

"I don't know. My two friends said there was someone here who found their way out but ended up back in This Place."

"So someone did notice," Emma says. She snorts and blows her hair out of her face. "This is why I like the Small Part. Nobody to bother me. Nobody to gossip. Nobody to ask,

How did you find your way? Not that it really matters, right? Did I really find my way if I just ended up back here?"

"But how did you?" Henry presses. "What was it like when you left This Place?"

Emma glares at her. "Not you too!"

Henry just stares up at her, and she eventually rolls her eyes.

"Fine. I don't really know, okay? It must not be what I thought, because I've tried to do it again this second time, and it doesn't work."

"What were you doing the first time?"

"I was walking by the beach." She sighs. "I was thinking about my father. I was remembering a time when I was small and we were packing for a trip. And my father told me that all the things I needed wouldn't fit in the bag. *Pack light*, he said. It was such a small thing, that memory. But the next thing I knew I was back in Joliet, in the meadow behind the house I was raised in. Pockets full of dried leaves. Alone."

"You don't know how you got back?"

"One minute my toes were wet in the sand; the next they were standing on dandelions."

"And you don't know what made it happen? Why that memory?"

Emma stops climbing again, looking up at the sky.

"I think it wasn't that I learned something in This Place— it was that I learned something about what I learned that day with my father."

"And what did you learn?"

"That sometimes people change," she says. She sounds far away, and Henry holds her breath, thinking Emma might disappear again right in front of her. She even looks a little faint against the sky. "And sometimes they never, ever will."

It must have been the strange glow of the nonfire, because now she looks solid again. Solid and definite. Here.

"Some people leave," Emma says. "But that doesn't mean they've found *the* way. Just *their* way. I'll tell you, I'm pretty sure people have left This Place having learned the wrong thing, do you hear me? But we're different every day of our lives. Or can be. You don't always have to feel lost to be found."

Both hands finally rest on the roof now, and then she slowly crawls her way up. This Place has many obscure rules, because once Emma is on the roof, she has no trouble walking along the steep slant of the roof toward the weather vane. As she said, it's toppled over, bent under a big branch.

"Your father made a choice on his way out of here," she calls down. "I don't know what it was. But we all make choices, and some of them only ever happen in our mind— that doesn't mean they can't knock over dominoes, though."

She wraps her hands around the weather vane and wrestles with it.

"What did my dad need to learn?" Henry calls back. "If there's some big thing we have to figure out before we get out, what was his?"

"Shouldn't you be asking about what *you* need to learn?" Emma cries. "Joseph is already home, isn't he? And you're here!"

Henry swallows. She's right. But Henry isn't just *here*— she's where her father was. If she leaves without finding out what made him lost to begin with—let alone found—she has a strong, sad feeling that she'll never actually know him. This is a place where she can uncover secrets. She feels it.

Emma seems to read her mind in the silence. When Henry looks up at the roof between the rungs of the ladder, Emma is standing upright with her eyes locked on her.

"Did they tell you about the Fountain of Truth?" she asks. "Where you can go and ask for answers?"

"A fountain? What kind of answers?"

"It's the only place in This Place where you can get the truth. But don't waste it asking about your father. You can only ask one thing. One. If you want out of here, focus on yourself."

But even as Henry nods, she knows she's going to ask about her father. She doesn't even know what the fountain is, or how it works. She doesn't even know exactly what she will ask. But whatever path her father was on, she is on too. It feels inevitable, like watching the line of a firework race up into the sky, knowing there will be a burst of color at the end.

Suddenly the air is filled with the sound of wolves howling. At home it might have made Henry jump, but she thinks This Place must have already changed her, because she looks around eagerly. Up in the sky above the Small Part, two suns shine off in the distance.

"Ah, they've come looking for you," she says. "You've already made friends."

"Those must be Wolfson's parents," Henry says to herself.

"The wolves are good people. Not people, you know. But however it works. The wolves have the right idea."

"Are you going to come and talk to them? To everyone?"

"No way. I only want to talk to one person, and he's not out there."

Emma turns away, back to the weather vane. She takes the nail and then pulls a hammer from a hidden pocket of her dress. Was she wearing a dress before? It looks like a child's dress—flamingo print. Short and flippy. With the hammer in hand, she pounds the nail into place, and when she finishes, the weather vane stands straight, its tip piercing upward.

"How do I get out of the Small Part?" Henry asks.

"Easy. You just walk."

"Which way?"

Emma jerks the weather vane into its final position, glances around, and then gives it one last twist. Then she points its silver arrow off into the woods.

"That way."

Henry frowns. Sadness settles into her. Though she barely knows Emma and has been here for only an hour, it feels like leaving someone behind. Which she supposes she is. Not just leaving her in this little slanted house, but leaving her on her journey.

Emma seems to read Henry's mind again.

"We make choices again and again and again. We can only make the ones we're ready to make, though. How long was your father gone?"

"At home it was a year."

"Then you'd better hurry back."

Henry steps away from the house, toward the woods where the weather vane points. The howling of Wolfson's parents sounds like thunder in the sky. But Henry knows it's just because she's small. Or because they're large. Whichever.

Then she pauses again.

"What about you getting down? I need to hold the ladder."

Emma waves her hand, staring up in the sky at where the moon should be. In the distance, Henry sees the torches of her friends, the people who have come to find her.

"I'll find my way."

Tears drip off Henry's chin as she stumbles through the dark in the direction Emma pointed. Henry slaps them away, and around her the trees get smaller and smaller. Or she gets bigger and bigger. She doesn't worry about the beasts now, with so many torches ahead. So why is she crying? A memory strikes hot across her brain—hiking with her father. Years ago when she was small. It was eighty-three degrees, and Henry was out of water.

"Make sure you don't cry." He laughed. "It attracts bears! You should've saved some of your water. We'll be back at the car soon, and you can rest."

"I'm thirsty. I didn't think it would be this long!"

"How long did you think ten miles is?" he teased. "You can't drink all your water halfway through!"

But he stopped by the side of the path and let her take a long drink from his bottle. That single sun burned in her eyes as she stared up at her dad and watched him look back the way they had come, down from the mountain.

"What?" Henry asked, still panting.

"Nothing," he said. "I just wish every day was like this."

"Hot?"

He laughed. "Yes, hot. But you here with me. Exploring together. Let's do this more. Let's make it a weekly thing. Okay?"

She remembers the feeling of his smile. Smiling at her with the same one he gave the mountains. So she said: "Okay." Even if in her head she heard, *Oh no.*

Then he recorded a video, and Henry felt a little embarrassed when he repeated how she drank all her water too soon. But at least they were there together. At least she was part of it. Wasn't she?

Now, making her way through the forest, she keeps her hand on the pouch—inside, two papers with his handwriting. He loved it here. He wanted to come back. It makes her chest ache.

"Henry!" She hears her name being called, louder and louder. "Henry, where are you?"

Henry is still in the dark, but the torches are just ahead. She stumbles forward out of the trees, which are quickly becoming bushes.

It's Ndidi. When Henry gets closer, she can see her face is streaked with tears.

"I'm here," Henry calls. Her voice sounds croaky. "I'm here."

"There she is!" Ndidi cries. She rushes forward. "She's okay!"

She stops just in front of Henry, like she'd been thinking about hugging her but stopped herself.

"You ran off by yourself, and then it got dark so fast. We could hear the beasts from far off. We thought...we thought..."

Behind her, Wolfson stands between his parents. His face is dry but pinched.

"I found the person who's been here twice," Henry says. She doesn't know why she says it, but she does.

"Emma," Wolfson says.

"Yeah."

"I can't believe you ran off by yourself," Ndidi says. Her tears are still flowing, but she looks angry now. "With beasts around? Why did you do that?"

Henry can't tell if she really wants an answer. How does she tell her that she knows her father is at home, but somehow she's looking for him here?

"I don't—" Henry begins, but Ndidi interrupts.

"We need to get back to the hostel," she says. "People are worried."

She walks away, still sniffling. Henry wants to say *I'm sorry*. She would say it three times: *I'm sorry, I'm sorry, I'm sorry*. But the words won't come out. The map is in her pack, and the guilt is in her stomach, and her tongue might as well be the X on her father's map.

X marks an empty place.

CHAPTER 16

enry has never woken to the sound of a baby before, but back in the hostel, the suns are barely up when the baby in the basket by Ndidi's bed starts to snuffle. Henry has heard all kinds of baby animals cry—dogs, kittens, even a baby tiger once when her father was invited to a special event at the zoo and took her along. This baby could be any one of them. Its little whimpers are low and muffled, and Ndidi hasn't stirred yet. Henry sits up in bed to see them both better—Ndidi's face curved into a soft frown.

Henry slips out of bed—barely catches her pack before it slides out of her sheets and hits the floor. She doesn't remember sleeping with it. It's near her pillow, the way a teddy bear might be. Inside is the map. The other odds and ends minus the nail. And the note, written with her father's tiny pencil. She almost pulls it out to read it again, to see if she can make the words feel different.

The baby fusses, a little louder now. Henry leans down to pick it up and realizes she's not sure how. The baby looks so small and vulnerable. She's sometimes hesitant to pick up a taco, afraid the shell will break, that everything inside will come pouring out. The stakes are much higher with a baby. But she wants Ndidi to sleep after how upset she was last night. She'd come back to her bed after finding Henry with the wolves and turned to face the wall.

In the end Henry just picks up the whole basket, and the rocking motion of hoisting it up seems to soothe the baby. Henry carries it out of the room and down the hall, then down to the kitchen, choosing the ramp this time so she doesn't jostle the baby. No matter what time of day, someone is always in the kitchen. Newly lost people are still on the clock of wherever home is—sometimes it takes a few days to adjust. That hadn't been the case for Henry. Her mother always said she could sleep anywhere.

"Hungry?" Mr. Javier says over the steam of a big pot when Henry appears. "I'm making sopa. A couple of the little kids have colds. Or at least they act like they do. Probably just homesick."

"Is homesick like actual sick here?"

"I think it's like actual sick anywhere," he says, and goes on stirring. Then he sees the basket she carries and smiles. "Baby-sitting today?"

"Ndidi was pretty upset last night. I wanted her to get some rest."

"Very considerate. I hear you met Emma."

"Yeah."

"Only person I know of who's been here twice."

Henry nods. "Do you think she just likes it here?"

"I haven't talked to her enough to know. And not in quite some time. But I would say anyone who stays in This Place for as long as Emma isn't here because they like it but because they're avoiding something." He pauses, thinking. "Except maybe Wolfson."

"What about Angie? She has to have been here a long time if she knows everything, right?"

Through the steam rising from the pot, Henry thinks his eyes get a little sad.

"Even Angie," he says. "And . . . well, even Angie."

A mewling sound floats from the basket.

"I think she's hungry," Henry says.

"No. Teething," Mr. Javier says. He takes up his knife and a raw carrot, peeling it deftly. Then holds it out to Henry. A moment later the baby is gumming it, staring up at the ceiling with wondering eyes.

"And you?" Mr. Javier says. "Are you hungry?"

"Kinda. But it doesn't matter, does it? Since we don't need to eat?"

"Does it matter," he scoffs, laughing lightly. "You think I only cook because you kids are hungry? I cook for my heart as well as your stomachs. Request something."

Henry switches the basket from hand to hand gently, so the baby can feel something different. Her house isn't a cooking house anymore. It's barely an eating-together house. She thinks she's eaten more meals in the car in the past year than at the dining room table.

"Have you ever heard of bean pie?" Henry asks. She never had until she met Ibtihaj, but Mr. Javier's eyes light up.

"There was a poet who came to my city once, a poet all the way from Harlem. He read from the Quran and told me stories about his home. He also told me about bean pie. We had most of the things he needed right there in Guaynabo, and so we made it together. *More or less*, he said. *More or less the same.* I remember how smooth it tasted. We had to use coconut milk. It tasted perfect. Perfect to *me*. I've never had it any other way. Isn't it funny how that works? I have gone all these years with an idea of what bean pie tastes like, because it's the only version I know. And your idea is probably completely different."

He smiles down into the pot. For a moment Henry thinks he forgets she's there.

"Let's make it," he says. "I haven't thought about the poet in a long time."

The beans aren't the same, he says, but they will work with what they have. He talks as he works.

"I don't know how long I've been here, but perhaps it has been for the best. I've wandered all over This Place and tasted everything I could find that didn't look deadly. I don't even know if anything here *is* deadly."

"Except the beasts?" Henry says.

"Well, maybe so."

Henry cracks three eggs into a bowl. The baby is still gumming the carrot, sitting in the basket on the counter and watching them.

"What kind of eggs are these?" Henry asks. The shells are light brown with darker brown spots.

"Not sure," he says. "Lost birds. We don't have those birds in Puerto Rico. But they're eggs."

He lets her pour things in, telling her when to add more.

"I've been in and out of Christopher's place," he says. "But haven't been able to find any measuring spoons. I've been eye-balling it for years."

"Years," she repeats. She thinks about years. About not seeing Ibtihaj for years. Or her mother.

"Or however long, since time is so strange here," he says, chuckling. He holds up a light brown stick. "This is like

181

cinnamon. I found a whole grove of it shortly after I got here, wandering This Place looking for a way out. Did you know if you walk away from the town and straight through the Wolf Woods and don't stop, that eventually you come out into a meadow, and if you keep going straight you run right back into the town again?"

"So This Place is ... round?"

He smiles broadly. "Could be," he says. "Or maybe folded? We'll never figure it out. But it is beautiful, I've found. And I've seen a lot of it."

"Have you heard of the Fountain of Truth?" she asks him. He stirs the batter, using a spring welded to a screwdriver as a whisk.

"Sure," he says. "That's one thing I haven't actually seen, though. I will say ... I've avoided it. It feels like a trick. How many people have found their way out of This Place after going and getting their one truth?"

She stares at him, waiting.

"None!" He laughs. "No one goes to the fountain and then, *poof*, gone. Don't you think everyone would be going if it worked like that?"

Henry shrugs, thinking of Emma. Emma said to focus on herself, on finding her own way. But the map showed the fountain, which meant her father had been there. Getting home is only as important as getting home to tell her father she followed in his footsteps. Getting home matters only if she's the right kind of daughter when she arrives. She turns to Javier.

"Can I ask you a question?"

"Sure."

But Henry pauses, remembering what Emma said. Her father not being well liked. Once, Henry overheard her mother on the phone with a therapist. *A friend of mine's daughter is having trouble getting over the loss of her father. I think my friend needs some help with how to handle it.* The daughter was Henry, the mother was her own. Her mother had a problem, but to talk about it, it needed to belong to someone else.

"I think my friend's dad was in This Place," she says to Javier. "Did you ever meet anyone named Joseph while you've been here?"

"Joseph…"

"Or Joe?"

"Hmm. I can't say I ever met a Joseph. Faces are like water to me. I remember their temperature, but the rest just slides on by. Especially names." He laughs a little at that. "Once upon a time I would've written that down."

He sees that she looks disappointed and tucks the laugh away.

"Not a face or a name. But what was he like?"

"Well, um, while he was here he was making a map?"

Henry swallows. She's spent so much of the past year not saying anything at all. This felt like lying in a way. Never quite answering her therapist's questions when she was asked how she was feeling. Avoiding her mother so they didn't have to talk. In that way Henry realizes she and her mother are the same—both of them avoiding saying *I'm okay* or *everything is fine* so they don't have to lie.

"*Oh*, the man with the map!" Javier says. "I do remember the man with the map. I'm sure the bees do as well."

"The bees?"

"Yes. You've seen the tall, tall tree between the market and the beach? At home I would've called it a kapok tree, but I'm sure it's called something else here, even if they look the same."

Henry nods so she doesn't have to say that she has not, in fact, noticed the tree. It's the sort of thing her father wouldn't miss. How can she make her brain work like his, if he is a butterfly and she is an earthworm? Can an earthworm grow wings?

"Well, the man with the map climbed a lot of trees while he was here. To get the lay of the land, you see."

Henry nods. That was her father. He had broken both arms climbing trees by the time he was eight. Henry never tried for precisely this reason.

"Well," Javier goes on. "That particular tree is home to a colony of bees. I wish I could tell you what kind because you seem like the kind of kid who wants to know. But all I know is they're the kind with a hive, and their hive is halfway up that tree. You're wondering why I'm telling you about the bees?"

Henry is not. She's thinking about the hive. Yes, her father definitely climbed that tree. And like the nail from the Small Part, he took a memento when he climbed down and placed it in his pack.

"Well, the mapmaker," Javier goes on. "He tells Angie that he's going to climb the tree to get a good view. And Angie tells him, not without asking the bees first, you're not. Well, the mapmaker had only been here a week or so, but he laughed a lot about the idea of asking the bees anything. So he climbed the tree with his things for mapmaking. And when he gets up there, well..."

"Did they sting him?" Henry asks quickly. Her father isn't allergic, but the idea of him being swarmed by a colony of bees makes her heart squeeze.

"No!" Javier gasps. "Oh no. They wouldn't do that. But they considered it very rude. I remember them gossiping about it for weeks."

Not well liked, Henry thinks. Her cheeks burn, and she hopes Mr. Javier doesn't notice.

"She's getting tired," Javier says, nodding to the baby in the basket. "Carry her."

Henry looks at the baby, who is still gumming the carrot. Henry almost forgot about her.

"How can you tell?" Henry asks. "She's not yawning."

"Look at her eyes. Seeing nothing. Pick her up."

Henry goes to pick up the basket, but Javier shakes his head.

"In your arms. She will sleep."

Henry thinks again of a taco, the shell breaking and everything falling out. When she moves to pick up the baby, the little one raises her arms, ready. Henry thinks she feels her heart turn into candle wax. Picking up the baby feels like the riskiest thing she's ever done. It feels the same as balancing on a window ledge. But the baby drops her head down against Henry's shoulder, her eyes still staring blankly.

"Walk her," Javier says. "You've seen babies be walked?"

"Kinda." But Henry walks. Back and forth along the island in the big kitchen.

"Sway a little," says Javier, and moves like he's dancing to a slow rhythm.

Henry walks and sways, and he nods approvingly.

"Me, the oldest of six boys," he says. "And always worrying about them all. Even the rough ones. I wish this child's parents could know that their baby is being walked and swayed, even in the land of the lost. It would be a comfort."

Henry can feel the baby go to sleep. Her body gets heavier and heavier. Heavier than Henry thought such a little person could be.

"You can put her in the basket now," he says.

"It's okay."

"I already have the crust made," he says. "I never seem to run out of dough in This Place, and the oven never cools."

Henry sways and watches him press the sun-colored dough into the dish. She thinks of Ibtihaj doing this with her family while Henry and her mother waited in the hospital with her father. Emma said there's nothing you can bring back from This Place when you find your way home. And the nail and the fragment of beehive didn't make it to her world. But Henry's father brought the necklace. She tells herself this is why she needs to go to the fountain. It has to tell her something. Something like an answer. Or a path to one.

"Into the oven it goes," Javier says. Henry is afraid the rattle of the door will wake the baby, but her breaths are long and deep. Henry watches him clean up the counter.

"What was the poet's name?" Henry asks. "The one from Harlem."

"Kalief," he says. "He wrote such beautiful poems. He loved the woodpeckers and coquí. He said if there were no animals in poetry, then it wasn't worth reading."

"Is he still in Puerto Rico? Or was he? When you got lost?"

"No. He left a long time ago. We lost touch."

"Oh."

"People move around," he goes on. "Or grow. Have fights. Misunderstandings. Distractions. New friends. New cities. You know what it's like to make new friends, don't you?"

"Kind of." She thinks of Ibtihaj. Once in fourth grade, Shane Bigelow kicked a soccer ball right into Henry's chest, and the idea of losing touch with Ibtihaj gives her that same achy pressure.

"I haven't thought of him in years," says Javier. "Not until you mentioned bean pie. Isn't that funny? The way something is buried in the sand until the ocean washes over it, and suddenly there it is . . . exposed to the light."

The sound of people calling to one another outside floats in through the open windows. The sound of waking. Henry wonders how long she's been up—after all, she's watched Javier make a whole bean pie.

"You really wouldn't go to the fountain?" Henry asks Javier. "Even if what it told you didn't send you home, don't you want to know what it would say?"

"Yes, of course," he says, wiping his hands on a towel. "But who's to say that what is true on one day will be true the next? Where is the truth coming from in the water? The past? The future?"

Henry doesn't know the answers to any of these things, but Javier doesn't look like he's actually asking her. He stares down at his hands, a little red from scrubbing the dough off them.

"I am forty-four years old," he says. "Or I was when I got lost. And even with this many years alive, I'm not sure how truth works."

He looks so sad all of a sudden. It makes Henry want to pass the baby to him, so he can feel the same warm weight that she does.

"Well, it's like you said," Henry says. "Things can change. Even if something isn't true tomorrow, that doesn't mean it wasn't true today. Right?"

"Yes," he says, smiling softly. "If that means the truth can change, that means we can change it ourselves, doesn't it?" He raises his eyes to Henry. He doesn't look sad anymore. But Henry thinks he's looking through her.

"Do you smell the pie?" he asks her.

She inhales. The smooth cinnamon smell fills the air of the kitchen.

Javier's eyes are looking far away, somewhere she can't reach. And then it's not just his eyes. Javier looks like a memory, a photograph faded in the sun. His hands hold the edge of the counter, and the expression on his face is of someone staring at the top of a hill, knowing something wonderful is about to appear from the other side, one inch at a time.

"Do you smell that?" he says quietly, with the same hopeful face. "I haven't smelled that since..."

And then Javier is gone.

CHAPTER 17

The baby is sleeping in the basket when Henry takes the pie out of the oven. It has speckles on its surface, just like the eggs she added to the batter. But it smells right and good, and she sets it on the counter just as Ndidi rushes down the stairs, another baby in her arms. This one is wailing.

"This one doesn't just want to be held," she cries over the noise. "Fast, what's ready? No, not pie. Any of the seed milk left? That will be okay. Warm it now, quickly."

The seed milk is still by the oven where Javier left it, and Henry fumbles to pour some into a jar. Ndidi gives her directions for warming it in a pot of water. Soon after, the infant is sucking it off Ndidi's finger.

"That's better," Ndidi says to the baby. "That's better, isn't it? Such crying. You'd think he understood This Place. Probably misses his mama."

The baby in the basket has woken now, too, and makes a coughing cry sound. Henry sighs and picks her up. Ndidi smiles.

"I miss my sisters," she says. "Never thought I would."

"Why?"

"They get so much," is all she says.

This is such a small part of what she really means. When Ndidi thinks of her sisters, she thinks of their laughter in the yard outside the door. When she thinks of them, her eyes hurt from always watching them. Her mother had praised her for this: *Ndidi, you have eyes in the back of your head!* It makes the back of her head hurt a little now too. When she thinks of her sisters, she again hears her mother's voice: *Ndidi, watch the babies while I go shopping. Watch your sisters while I take this meeting.* She feels hungry.

"Where's Javier?" Ndidi says, because everything else is too big to say. "I was going to request akara and pap for breakfast. Oh, look, beans are already set out. I wonder if he's made it before, or something like it. Where is he, anyway?"

"Well...," Henry starts, but she's not quite sure how to finish. "He was, um, here, and we were talking, and we made the pie, and the baby slept, and he was standing there, and then he started looking a little different, and then...I don't know? He disappeared. So I guess that means...?"

191

"Javier found his way?" Ndidi gasps. "Here? This morning?"

She hurriedly sets the baby in the basket on the floor and rushes to Henry's side.

"Here? Where? There, by the stove? What was he doing when it happened? What did he say?"

Henry describes everything that happened, and Ndidi mirrors the movements.

"Like this?" she says. "And he...what? Smelled the pie?" She inhales deeply, wafting some of the cinnamon air into her nose. "Like that?"

Henry watches her moving around, trying to put her feet where Javier's were. After a moment, Ndidi stops, looks down at her sandals.

"I didn't think it would work," she says. "But I...hoped it would. The thought of going home right now and having akara and pap..." She trails off. Then her eyes widen.

"Oh no," she says. "With Javier gone, who is going to make breakfast for the kids? They're going to be waking up soon!"

"We don't really *need* to eat, remember?" Henry says quietly.

Ndidi gives her a sharp look.

"They're little, Henry," she says. "It's not the same for them. They may not *need* it, but they need it."

"I—"

"So what are you going to make?"

"Me?"

"Sha, you should've already started, honestly. When Javier found his way, did you not think about the little kids? They'll be down soon. So what can you make?"

"I... don't really cook at home."

Ndidi darts around to Henry's side of the counter, yanking open the cold box.

"Eggs," she says. "So many eggs. You can do *something* with eggs."

Then she's turned away, back to the babies, leaving Henry staring down at the dozens of speckled eggs and all the tools that were left out when Javier disappeared. She begins to crack eggs. She stirs them clumsily.

"Your parents didn't teach you to cook?" Ndidi says curiously, watching her make a mess of cracking eggs.

Henry picks yet another piece of eggshell out of the bowl.

"We're kind of a cereal house."

"You have nothing but time here to learn," Ndidi says. "Sometimes doing things ourselves is the best way. My mother always says repeating other people's mistakes is one thing, but no one likes to repeat their own."

She stares pointedly at the shattered eggshell in Henry's hand. Henry begins to laugh.

"So tell me how to do it!"

"What did I just tell you?" Ndidi grins. "Learn yourself. But at least try a different technique o."

But she comes around the counter to show her. Together they watch the babies in their baskets, and they crack lots and lots of eggs. Henry can feel Ndidi forgiving her. Together they relax. By the time the little kids come down, the two of them, laughing, have managed to make something like a large flat omelet. Ndidi recommended a baking dish instead of a frying pan. Together they peered at it after pulling it from the oven, Ndidi sprinkling it purposefully with what looks like ground pepper from the tiny wooden bowls Javier kept on the tables.

The kids cry when they learn he's gone.

"But he was going to make me French toast," one boy sniffles. "He's not coming back?"

"He has to come back," another kid wails. "Why isn't he here?"

"He found his way home," Ndidi says soothingly. "That's what we want for each other. Javier went home. That's what we all want."

Except for Emma, Henry thinks. But as she looks out the window, she catches sight of the tall, tall tree that Javier spoke of. *The bees*, she thinks. She didn't ask Emma if she stayed because she had things she needed to do. Henry has things she needs to do.

Wolfson appears, as he so often does. This Place makes him quiet in a different way than home makes Henry.

"What did Javier cook?" he asks, peering around at everyone's plates. He looks suspicious.

"Henry made this, actually," Ndidi says.

"Hey!" Henry cries. "Not just me."

"But what *is* it?" he says, truly curious. Henry wonder if being raised by wolves means he doesn't understand humor like other people do.

"Food," Ndidi says. "That's all."

"Did Javier not want to cook today?"

Ndidi's smile fades a little then. "He found his way this morning. Right in front of Henry."

"Oh." Wolfson swings his eyes onto Henry. "Was he afraid?"

"No. Why would he be afraid?"

"Some people are when they find their way."

"You've seen it happen?"

"Yes, during my time here." He glances at Henry sideways. "Haven't spent much time in the Small Part, though."

Henry's face heats. She should apologize, and apologies are hard. Harder when there are so many things she still can't say.

"About last night," she begins. "Sorry. For acting like that at Christopher's. For making everybody worry."

"Next time have some sense o. Getting even more lost in a lost place is bad enough, but there are monsters out there now. The beasts."

Henry hasn't told them that the beasts are what chased her to the Small Part. When she was found, Wolfson's parents silently brought her and Ndidi back to the hostel. Then Ndidi was in her bed with her back turned.

Henry tells them now, quietly so the little kids don't hear. How the beasts stalked her through the trees, chased her until she couldn't breathe. But she doesn't tell them how the beasts stared at her when she reached Emma. There's a sinking feeling when she thinks of it. How they stared like they knew her.

"And the lonely woman saved you? What's her name again?" Ndidi asks.

"Emma," Henry answers. "Yes, she did. She told me about the Fountain of Truth too. Do you know about it?"

"Of course," Wolfson says.

"What's that?" Ndidi says, leaning forward.

"One of the magic places," Wolfson says.

"One of?" Henry says. "Isn't this whole place magic?"

He frowns a little more. "If you believe a witch runs everything, yes. Don't know whether it's hers or not, but the Fountain of Truth is magic."

"What about the Small Part? That seemed like magic. And Christopher too."

"What's the difference between magic and curse?" Ndidi says.

"The Fountain of Truth," Wolfson interrupts, "will tell you one truth."

"What kind of truth?"

He shrugs. Now would be a good time for Henry to tell them what Javier said about why he'd never been to the fountain. But instead, she says:

"I want to go."

Ndidi looks at her with bright eyes.

"You think it will tell you something that will help you go home?" she says.

"Yes," Henry says. This is partially true.

Ndidi turns to Wolfson. His face is cloudy.

"Come with us," Ndidi says, grabbing his shoulder and jiggling it.

"I don't like the idea of it," he says.

"Why?"

"How can water tell me something I don't know myself?"

Henry remembers the year Ibtihaj broke her arm. She begged not to go to the doctor. *What if they say it's broken?!* It was. But even with the pain, it felt better not knowing. Wolfson's face tells Henry he might be thinking something similar.

"It's not just any water," Ndidi says. "It's water *here*. Come on. Maybe it will tell you something that can help you understand what's going on with This Place. The beasts and the bats and all those things. The moon. Maybe the fountain can help."

The clouds remain, but this changes his mind. Wolfson is thinking about Angie, and Daughter. He's thinking about how his parents have no moon to howl at. For Henry's part, she thinks of her father and the stories she will tell when she sees him. She imagines tapping every place on the map, explaining to him she's seen what he's seen. The necklace feels heavy around her neck. She's holding it in her hand when, outside, it begins to snow.

All the little kids run to the window, amazed. The snow seems to come from nowhere and go nowhere. It doesn't land, just floats in the air, disappearing and reappearing.

"See?!" Ndidi cries, gesturing at the window. "You have to come with us, Wolfson."

He's already decided he will go, but still has arguments to make. Henry slips away from the table.

The snow makes her think of the beasts—their whiteness, their coldness. She remembers the way saliva made their lips glitter as she held the necklace in her palm. She hopes the trip to the fountain will be short, that it can be finished in daylight. But just in case, she climbs the stairs back to her room, lifts the necklace over her head, and tucks it under the pillow. Without it, her neck feels lighter. When she gets back down to Ndidi and Wolfson, the snow is gone and they're ready to leave.

CHAPTER 18

They find Angie at her stall. She's just finished giving the welcome speech to a new lost person, a tall, tall woman wearing a basketball uniform. The woman looks dazed. Angie gives the woman's back a quick rub before the woman sets off toward the hostel.

"Wolfson," Angie says, her expression brightening when she sees him.

"Did you hear Javier found his way?" he says quickly.

Her eyes widen. "I didn't. Oh! This morning? I just saw him last night!"

"In the kitchen before breakfast," Henry says. "We were talking about pies, and then he was gone."

"Sometimes it's the little things," she says. She looks

somewhere between sad and happy, but not envious as Ndidi had. She turns her eyes to Henry. "I'm glad you're okay after your adventure yesterday."

She doesn't mean it in a mocking way, but Henry still feels embarrassed.

"I met Emma."

"I thought you might," Angie says, nodding. "People have a way of ending up in the Small Part when they're feeling very small. Now what are you three up to?"

"We want to go to the Fountain of Truth," Ndidi says shyly. "Can you give us directions?"

We don't need directions, Henry thinks. Not with the map her father made. She could say something right now. Show them and tell them. But no one else talks about their families. Ndidi and her little crumbs about her mother that she seems to wish she ate instead of saying out loud. Henry stays quiet while Angie begins to weave a rope of the purple flowers, studying Wolfson.

"Are you hoping to come across something that will help you find your way?" she asks him. "Is there something you want to ask it?"

Wolfson lifts his chin.

"That's not why I want to go," Wolfson answers. "I want to ask it about what's going on in our world. And besides, I don't want them going alone."

Angie's shoulders relax, so slightly only her shirt and Henry notice.

"I see."

Ndidi pipes up. "Well, figuring out how to find my way is exactly why *I* want to go."

Angie smiles, spreading it out among the three of them.

"I understand wanting to check it out," she says. "But don't have your heart set on a shortcut. Be prepared for a detour."

She's silent a moment, she and Wolfson sharing a look. It makes Henry ache. When was the last time her mother looked at her this way? Looked at her at all? She suddenly feels like shouting: *My dad was here. Don't you understand? Don't you see how important this is?* But now Angie has let the flower chain drop and points toward the Pepper Sea.

"You have to go far down the beach, where it meets the Salt River. Remember when I took you to the Salt River?" Wolfson nods. "Good. Follow the river until you get to the sandbox. Cross it, then follow the dragonflies from there. There will be mangroves, but if they start to go uphill, you've gone too far. You're going now?"

Wolfson nods again. Henry is thinking about the Salt River. Was that on her father's map?

"Be careful," Angie says. "Be back before the suns go down."

"We will."

"You will, right?" she says, her lips curving up. She is sure of him, and he is sure of her.

"Yes." He smiles back. And then he and Henry and Ndidi go.

They keep an eye on the suns, knowing they can't be trusted. In Henry's pack, the map travels with them. She doesn't have the urge to peek at it until they're nearing the far end of the beach and Ndidi remarks on the tall, tall tree.

"You can't even see the top. I bet if you climbed up there you could see this whole place. Then we'd know how long until we get to this Salt River Angie spoke about."

"I've been a couple times. It's not far."

It crushes Henry a little. When she sees a tree like this, she studies its bark. She looks for small, slow, unusual things—a letter carved in or a trail of serious ants. It does not occur to her to climb trees. Does not occur to her that reaching the top may reveal something. But it does to Ndidi. It does to her father.

"Do you hear the bees?" Wolfson asks. "Every bee in This Place lives here."

Henry is thinking about what Javier told her about her father. A very tall tree between the beach and the market. This has to be it. She moves off the path, closer to the tree, and

202

rests her palm against its trunk. Branches jut out in a spiraled fan, all the way to the top. She rests her foot on the lowest.

"I'm going to go up," she says.

"Why?" Wolfson sounds surprised.

"Why not?" It's something her father would say. It makes her feel brave to say it. She has never climbed a tree in her life.

"It's too tall, Henry, no," Ndidi says, sounding doubtful.

Wolfson's surprise and Ndidi's doubt only push Henry to climb. This is how an earthworm like her grows wings, she thinks, peering far up into the sky. And if not wings, feet.

She brings her other foot onto the branch.

"You should at least ask the bees," Wolfson says flatly.

"Hey, bees," Henry calls up into the leaves.

The three of them wait in silence.

"No one home." Henry grins.

She grips the next branch, climbing hand, then foot. The tree is perfect for climbing—almost like Emma's ladder, straight and stacked. Stronger, though. Henry feels more confident as she goes. The higher she gets, the more she feels like she could climb forever.

The wind tickles her neck. The leaves are too thick to see through, but they look thinner above. She looks only up, never down. The wind against her neck. It whispers in her ear.

No higher, the wind says.

"Okay?" Wolfson calls from far below. He sounds small. The wind is closer. It tickles her neck.

Not the wind.

She sees the first bee on her knuckles. Her heart and her hand both flutter, and the bee takes off. Another lands on her wrist.

No higher, says the wind that is not the wind.

Bees. More and more of them. They're silent, not buzzing or humming. The branches above Henry darken, as if a cloud is passing over. But the cloud is the bees, and they swarm softly around her. In a cartoon, they might pick her up and carry her away.

Go back, the bees tell her. *This is not for you.*

Henry's father was told this before. She remembers that day. The day he hiked six miles to avoid paying a Paiute toll and climbed the mountain on his own. *Not everything is for you*, people wrote under the video. That was when he bought the bag Henry carried: NATURE IS NEUTRAL.

"I just want to look around," Henry says. She has learned that swiping at bees is a bad idea. That's at home. Javier said they hadn't stung her father. But what if they change their minds?

You have no permission to be here, the bees say.

"I called up to ask."

What does no answer mean to you?

"Are you okay, Henry?" Ndidi calls. She and Wolfson have stood back away from the trunk, hoping to see her better. The foliage blocks their view.

"Yes!" she calls. But isn't actually sure.

Go back.

She can't now. She can't see This Place yet. Having the map in her pack doesn't feel like enough. She needs to see what he saw.

"My father came this way," she says. "I just...I need..."

Then your father is the mapmaker, the bees say.

"How did you know?"

No one else has climbed this tree.

He would be so proud of this. To do what no one else has done. In spite of bees. To have seen what no one else has seen.

This makes you proud? the bees ask.

Henry isn't sure if the bees can read her mind, but she holds very still as they begin to crawl down the length of her arm.

"Henry?" Ndidi shouts.

"I'm okay," Henry calls, because she is, she thinks, even as more and more bees appear to examine her.

Are you here to take from us? the bees ask.

"No," she says. In a way it feels like the first time she's been honest since she came to This Place.

Then what?

"I'm...I'm following the map."

Your father's map.

"Yes."

Why?

"Henry, what are you doing?" Wolfson calls. "We need to get to the fountain!"

The fountain, the bees say as they crawl on her hands, slowly and silently. *Then you're looking for something true.*

"I'm looking for my way home."

You're looking for your father.

"No, I know where he is."

What are you doing so high? Do you want to be a bird?

Henry's hands are beginning to sweat where they grip the branch. Her beating heart makes her say something she wouldn't usually say out loud:

"No, I want to be a butterfly."

But you are not a butterfly.

One of Henry's tears drips down onto the branch before it's covered by bees. To keep more from falling, she tilts her head back, staring up into the branches. Many branches above, she can make out the shape of hives. A dozen of them, some built against the trunk, some hanging from branches.

"I have something of yours," she tells the bees. Suddenly the pack around her waist is so heavy it feels like an anchor.

She reaches inside, and her fingers find the soft, dry piece of hive, as light as air and as soft as a feather.

She places it on the flat surface of the branch, and the bees immediately swarm over it. It's gone before she can blink.

This is ours, the bees say, and they sound pleased. *Thank you. How does it feel?*

"How does what feel?"

To step off the map?

"Henry, come down! We're going to run out of daylight!"

Go now, the bees say. *What you're looking for isn't up here.*

Climbing down is harder than climbing up. She wasn't worried about falling on the way up. Now, going down, she second-guesses every branch. Every foothold feels slippery. Letting go of the last one is hard—so hard she waits for what must be a long time, because Ndidi says, "You can just jump. You're so close."

"Are you sure?" Henry doesn't want to look down. She keeps looking up, even as the hives have gotten so small she can no longer see them.

"Yes, just let go and drop," Wolfson says.

Henry lets go. The drop feels long and wobbly, and when she lands, she stumbles.

"Are you okay?" Ndidi asks, steadying her. "You were up there so long! What did you see?"

"The bees."

"Were they mad?" Wolfson says, sounding alarmed.

"A little. But they didn't sting me."

She almost tells them then. Somehow the pack feels so much lighter now, without the bit of beehive in it. Even though it felt like paper in her hand. The bees said she was going off her father's map, and now she desperately wants to take it out and study it. She has seen the bees' tree for herself now. She climbed it as her father had climbed it. So what did the bees mean by going off the map?

"Let's keep going," Wolfson says. He's already moving off down the path. "Angie said we need to get to the Salt River, then follow it."

Ndidi falls into step next to him, with Henry a little behind. They walk like that for a while, quiet, each of them lost in their own thoughts. As it happens, they are each thinking of their mother. Wolfson, trying to remember the woman's face. Ndidi, wondering if she was missed only in moments when the babies needed looking after. Henry, thinking of the shelves in the basement and why her mother never went down. Because they reminded her of Dad, or because, like Henry, she found the ghostliness of the shells and antlers was too much?

"I hear the river," Ndidi says happily.

"Do you like rivers?" Henry asks.

"I love water. I always have."

"Not me," says Henry.

"Why do you two do this?" Wolfson asks when a moment of quiet passes.

"Do what?"

"Say the start of things, but not the end."

Henry and Ndidi exchange a look of confusion.

"You asked 'if' she likes water, but you didn't ask why. Don't you want to know why?" he says.

He says it in his usual flat way, and at home Henry might have thought he was being unfriendly. But he waits, glancing between them.

"It doesn't seem like something anyone wants to know," Ndidi says.

"I would," Henry says.

"Then why didn't you ask her?" Wolfson says, curious. Confused.

"Because...I don't know. I assume if someone doesn't say, then they don't want to be asked."

"Not saying because you think no one wants to hear," he says. "Not asking because you think no one wants to tell."

His voice sounds like he's doing math.

"Ndidi, why do you love water?" Henry asks.

Ndidi looks shy, the same way she did when Angie spoke to her and only her.

"Because it goes wherever it wants," she says.

"Then you're going to love the Salt River," Wolfson says, smiling.

The path bends to the right, and just beyond is the river itself. Now Henry sees what he meant.

"Angie says that in your world, salt in the water makes things float more. I don't know if there's salt in the Salt River or not, but the whole thing floats."

Henry stares with her mouth open, and Ndidi covers hers. The Salt River is like if water were sucked through an invisible straw, then held in midair. A floating, flowing current. It twists and turns, sometimes running inside a grounded riverbed, and in other places lifting high overhead. Ndidi runs to one of these floating places, gazing up.

"It doesn't even drip!" she cries. "How does it work?"

"It just does." Wolfson shrugs.

After spending a lifetime in This Place, Wolfson has seen the Salt River many times, but never with anyone new. He watches Ndidi stretch her arm up and graze the floating river, and he smiles. Henry watches him.

"Do you like water?" she asks.

"I can swim if I have to."

"But do you *like* it?"

"I don't know. Why don't you like it?"

"I think the same reason Ndidi likes it," she admits. "It can do whatever it wants."

Her father considers swimming part of survival training. But every time Henry touches water, she sinks like a stone. That she doesn't have to swim the river is a great relief.

"You two!" Ndidi cries. "Quick! Look!"

She sounds alarmed, and Wolfson and Henry are at her side in an instant. She's pointing up into the floating section of the river. On the other side are clouds and treetops. But Ndidi's finger aims inside the water.

The water is full of money.

Coins. Gold, silver, and copper. They tumble along with grains of sand, pushed by the current. They glitter in the light from the two suns, making the ground under the twisting river sparkle.

"Doesn't this answer our question?" Ndidi says, smiling. "About where lost money goes?"

Henry reaches up into the water, almost afraid she'll pop it like a balloon. Water flows down her arm, but the river keeps running. She grabs a handful of coins and withdraws her hand.

"I never thought to do that," Wolfson says. There's a smile in his voice, and the three of them bend their necks over her palm, looking at the coins. Henry recognizes none of them, and neither does Ndidi. Wolfson has to have coins explained to him. Henry divides the coins between them, and they take turns tossing them back into the river. Too hard and the coins pass straight through.

"Underhand," Henry says, and demonstrates.

"No one will ever believe me," Ndidi says when all the coins are gone and her hands are dry. "I wish I could show someone. My mother. I would just—" She pauses, then holds her thumb and finger on both hands up, like a camera. She clicks her tongue. "So she could see. If I ever get home."

"You will," Henry says. "We will."

Ndidi smiles a smile that isn't sure. But she nods anyway. "First, though," she says, "the sandbox. Right, Wolfson?"

"That's what Angie said."

"Have you been there, too?" Henry says.

The three of them duck under the floating river and carry on.

"Once or twice. It's not too far."

Henry wants more than ever to bring out the map. She doesn't remember seeing anything that looked like the Salt River marked. Has she seen something her father did not?

"Do you think we're dead?" Ndidi asks suddenly.

"Dead?" Wolfson says, surprised.

"Yes. Could we be? The dead don't know they're dead, do they?"

"We're not dead," Henry says. She knows for certain because of her father. But Ndidi doesn't know where the certainty comes from; she only hears it in her voice.

"How can you be sure?"

"I just am."

The sound of the floating river gets softer and softer as they go on.

"One thing I will miss from here," Ndidi says, "if I ever get home? The quiet."

Henry thinks of the quiet at home. Not the soft kind, but the heavy kind. All the space between her and her mother. It will be different now with her father home. He is not a quiet man. Even when he isn't talking, his videos are. Footage and the news. Henry wishes she had a map for that—the terrain of what home will be. How to navigate that new land?

"You're doing it again," Wolfson says. He swipes at a low-hanging vine. "Saying part of a thing."

Ndidi laughs.

"Sometimes I'm just thinking out loud o. Not everything has to be talked about."

But some things do, Henry can hear her therapist at home say. She said this in a joint session with Henry's mother. Henry's mother does not like talking about things.

"Maybe you can take the quiet home," Henry says. It's not a pine cone or even a piece of hive. But Henry imagines putting the feeling of climbing the bees' tree into her pocket and carrying it back through Quinvandel.

"What do you miss about home, Henry?" Wolfson asks.

"My collages."

She says it so fast that the guilt hits a second later. She should have said her mother. Or even her father.

"You're an artist," Ndidi says, sounding impressed. "Cool."

"I guess so. I mostly just...like it."

"There was an artist here for a while," Wolfson says. "They followed Mr. Javier everywhere to see where he got his spices. Then they would use some to make paint."

"Did they take their paintings home with them? What will people at home think of them!"

Again, the map. The red ink on the back that was invisible in Quinvandel, seen only in This Place. All the things Henry can't say. She sees why they call Emma the lonely woman. Keeping everything to yourself is quiet, and Henry thought she was tired of quiet.

"There it is," Wolfson says. "There's the sandbox."

CHAPTER 19

Henry doesn't know what she expected when Angie originally said *sandbox*, but ahead of them is an actual sandbox. The kind that looks like a child's toy: the green-turtle kind that, when the shell is lifted, contains sand and toy tools to build crumbly castles. Except this one is huge. The size of a football field.

"Wolfson, what...?" Ndidi starts.

"I had one of these," Henry says, in awe. "When I was little."

"One of what?" Wolfson answers, confused.

"A sandbox like that. The turtle kind."

Both he and Ndidi stare at her the way someone who hasn't yet swallowed the red berries of This Place would stare.

"A sandbox?" Henry asks. "Do they not have sandboxes in Nigeria? It's like—"

"Yes, we have sandboxes," Ndidi cries. "Do you think it is an alien planet?"

"No," she says, embarrassed. "I just thought...okay, sorry. I just mean, the turtle kind. Everybody has seen the turtle kind. Where I'm from, anyway. Just...not this big."

Wolfson studies the sandbox. His eyes look faraway.

"I think I kind of remember that...," he starts to say, but then he shakes his head. "Let's go ahead and get across. Who knows when the suns might change."

"Good point," Ndidi says. "Let's get going."

Henry wonders if Ndidi noticed the memory on his face before he pushed it away. She thinks it would be awkward to bring it up now. Wolfson and Ndidi scale the mound of dirt and sand that slopes up to the edge of the sandbox, and Henry follows.

At the top, they all stand motionless.

"Um," Ndidi says. "That's not sand."

"No," Henry says. "It's not."

Wolfson crouches down, reaching his hand in to scoop it up.

"Snow," he says.

"It's cold?" Ndidi says.

"Very cold."

"But the air isn't even cold! That doesn't make sense!" Henry says.

"What does in This Place?" Ndidi murmurs.

"It used to make more sense than this. This *used* to be sand," Wolfson says. That frown is back, the grandfather one that carries the whole world in its crease. "We need to get back and tell Angie about this."

"Now?"

"Yes. This is not right. A little snow outside the hostel is strange enough. But this?"

He shakes his head, looking more worried than ever.

"We can't go back now," Henry says. "We got to the sandbox. That means on the other side of this we just have to follow dragonflies to the mangroves! We're so close!"

All the talk about home has made her anxious. She thinks of what the fountain might tell her, and it almost makes her stomach ache.

"Something is wrong in This Place," Wolfson says, shaking his head. "Snow has replaced sand. It's so strange. Angie should know."

"We can still tell Angie," Henry says. "But can we please just do this first?"

"We can see the other side," Ndidi says quietly. "It won't take long."

She is thinking of home too. Home has become a fourth person on their journey.

Wolfson glances up at the sky again. None of them trust the suns.

"We'll be quick," Henry says.

She's the first to step in, and she sinks deeper than she thought she would. Ndidi laughs nervously, then sinks in next to her. The cold of it presses against Henry's stomach.

"I don't know about this," Wolfson says. But Ndidi and Henry are already wading forward, and a moment later he's there beside them.

"It's so cold," he says, shocked. "Why isn't it melting in the suns?"

"Do I need to say it again o? Nothing makes sense here."

They make their way slowly across the sandbox. It didn't look so far when they set out, and if it were still sand, it wouldn't have been. But wading through the snow is slow, and eventually Henry's teeth are chattering so hard she almost bites her tongue.

"May not have been so wise," Ndidi says. Her voice sounds slurred with cold.

Wolfson looks behind them. "Would take just as long to go back now."

"Are we going to freeze?" Ndidi says, sounding scared. "Foolish to freeze in the bright sun. Suns."

"Let's move faster," Henry says, but the snow is even deeper here in the middle of the sandbox, and the going is even slower. Henry's father never hiked cold places. *Let the snow guys handle the snow*, he said. Will she ever be able to tell him about this?

"I'm getting stuck, I think," Ndidi says. Around the chattering of her teeth, she sounds panicky.

"So am I," Wolfson says quietly.

Henry is a little taller than both of them, and she struggles forward but eventually feels stuck too. The snow is cold, and she's tired, and it's up around her chest.

"We have to go back," she says. "Along the path we've already made."

Wolfson nods in agreement, but when they turn to face the direction they came from, all they see is the smooth white surface of the snow. If they didn't feel the aching cold pressing around them, they might think it was a pristine beach.

"What . . . how?"

"Like we were never here," Wolfson says. "Like it doesn't remember us."

"Remember us?"

"This Place is funny about memories," he says. Henry thinks it sounds like something Angie would say.

You will freeze, says a voice, and Henry knows before she even looks around that they are being addressed by an animal.

A moose. Henry had an idea of how large moose are, but it wasn't an accurate picture. The animal is far more massive than she thought a moose would be, and it stands in the snow staring down at them. She thinks it feels royal somehow.

"Hello," Wolfson says. "Where did you come from?"

A place much colder than this, it says. *Where the sun is changing. Warmer and warmer. This is how I lost my way. Things are strange, different.* It pauses, giving the three of them a longer study. *Although not as strange as this. What are you doing? You are not made for this.*

"No, we're not," Ndidi says.

I am, it says.

Henry thinks the cold is making her brain slow. She doesn't know what they're going to do. The idea of the snow closing behind them like an ocean makes her feel stiff with terror. Or maybe that's the cold too. Has her father ever felt this way? Like the woods closed around him?

I will carry you, if you'd like. I think I can manage.

As it turns out, the moose can.

Climbing up is harder than Henry thought it would be. She's ridden a horse before, but only with a saddle. And a moose is so much bigger than a horse—she had no idea just how big. It has no problem carrying all three of them. On its back, Henry sits higher than in her father's pickup truck. The moose moves easily through the snow, like a plow with antlers.

I've never carried a person before, the moose says. *Another strange thing.*

"Just roll off," Wolfson says when they arrive at the other side of the sandbox, and they do, dropping back into the snow like melting icicles.

Is there a way out? the moose asks them when they're standing on the edge of the sandbox, out of the snow. The warmth from the suns sinks into Henry. She feels like she's thawing. *Of This Place?*

"Yes, but you have to find it," Wolfson says. "You have to find it in yourself."

I was born knowing the way, the moose says. *But my world is changing.*

"So is this one," Wolfson says.

Henry wants to tell it that her father saw moose once, a mother and her calf. He wasn't hiking, but in Montana for a meeting. He saw them out of the window of his shuttle. Henry asked to see a photo, but he hadn't taken one. He had, however, found a moose tooth on a hike and brought it home.

The three of them watch the moose move off across the snow. It's already vanished before Henry can even remember to say thank you.

CHAPTER 20

Angie was right about following the dragonflies. Once the three of them are clear of the sandbox—the snow box—the zooming jade clouds of insects lead them right to the Fountain of Truth, which is much less like a fountain and much more like a big puddle.

But *puddle* doesn't really do it justice. Henry's not sure what word would. The fountain is only about as big as a Hula-Hoop, but one look says that to dive in would mean never reaching the bottom. The blue is the color Henry thinks of when she thinks of Earth—a photo taken by an astronaut from space. Though the planet looks tiny in the photo, it also looks bigger than one could ever imagine. The puddle is this same way.

"It isn't what I thought it would be," Wolfson says.

"No," Ndidi agrees.

But no one says anything like *This isn't a fountain at all*, even if they think it. Something about the water forbids it. Henry studies its edges, looking for frogs or those bugs that skim across water. None. It's not that kind of water. When she stares at the center, it seems to blacken. She rubs her ears, like wind has tickled them or the bees are back.

Ndidi leans over and spits right into it.

"Ndidi!" Wolfson gasps. Henry's mouth drops open.

"I—I—" Ndidi stammers. She looks horrified, embarrassed.

"Why did you—"

"I had to, it was a feeling, I don't—"

But they all fall immediately silent when something in the water moves.

A bubble, rising from the impossible depths. They see it coming, the water stirring to make way for it. When it reaches the top, it has grown but doesn't burst at the surface. It waits there, like a shining dome.

Without saying a word, Ndidi slowly bends to it, then pokes it with her finger.

The bubble seems to kiss her fingertip. Then it narrows into a cylinder. The cylinder stretches into a string. A rope of water emerges from the surface of the pool, slowly at first, like a curious snake.

No one moves.

It rises, twisting slowly, wrapping itself into the air. Ndidi, still crouching, stares at it like she's been hypnotized. But she's smiling a little, one corner of her mouth tugged up in wonder. She tilts her head as it climbs higher. Then it's at her ear. It looks like it's whispering.

Wolfson and Henry exchange looks. His face has changed from when they set out—patient and a little sullen. But now he's here, and he's seen the water moving, and Henry can tell he's going to do it too. The question must be in the spit, because Henry feels it pulling her now. Saliva gathers in her mouth, like the feeling just before throwing up. The kind of spit that can't be swallowed.

They spit into the Fountain of Truth. First Henry and then Wolfson, and just like that, their own bubbles start to rise from the bottom—if there is a bottom. The bubbles peek up into the open air, like they're checking to be sure the two of them are sure. Henry is. Wolfson must be too. The bubbles become funnels, then strings, the snakiness of the water rising to each of their ears where they crouch at the edge.

Henry doesn't know what she expected to hear when the water reached her ear. She thought there would be a story, or a flash of memory. Something that answered the question she didn't even know she was asking.

Instead, when the waterspout comes close enough to whisper, it says only five words.

Your father is a thief.

The suns betray them again.

Or maybe this time, they betray the suns.

Henry has no idea how long they've been at the Fountain of Truth when Wolfson shakes her shoulder. She doesn't feel like she's been sleeping, but she does feel like she's been dreaming. Wolfson's face tells her he feels the same way. She looks around for Ndidi, and she's behind him, looking up at the sky, her head tilted way back. It's almost dark.

"Are you okay?" Wolfson asks Ndidi.

She just nods. She looks less dreamy than Henry feels. Wolfson looks at Henry, drops his chin to ask the same question.

"I guess so," she answers. "Did it tell you anything?"

He just shrugs, and when she asks Ndidi, she does the same thing. Henry feels what the fountain told her burning in her ear: *Your father is a thief.* So when Ndidi finally drops her eyes from the moonless sky and asks Henry what she heard, Henry shrugs too.

Silence makes them all islands now.

"We'll go around the sandbox on the way home," Wolfson says. "It may take longer, but it's worth it."

So they do, walking fast in an attempt to beat the setting suns. Walking along the perimeter of the sandbox is like edging a huge white desert. The snow doesn't even breathe cold the way the freezers do in grocery stores—Henry would never guess it wasn't sand unless she sank a foot in. She doesn't see the moose anywhere either. In her heart, she hopes that means it found its way that quickly.

"It wasn't always like this?" she says out loud as the sky dims. "The suns? The snow? The weird days?"

"No," Wolfson says. "It's always been a strange place, but it was never like this. It was never dangerous."

"Danger is everywhere," Ndidi says.

"Not here. Things in This Place can't hurt you," he says. "Angie told me that in her world—I mean, our world—she lost someone in the water once. They...drowned? In the water."

Henry is confused and doesn't reply at first.

"Okay?" she says eventually. "Yes, that happens."

"Not here," he says. "If you swim in the Pepper Sea, it will carry you back to shore. You see what I mean?"

"I think so."

"But the snow," he says. "It felt...dangerous?"

Henry nods. It did. Snow is dangerous wearing the clothes they're wearing. Though her father didn't do snow hikes, he still taught her about frostbite and hypothermia. *It doesn't even need to be snowing for your body to get dangerously cold*, he told her. *Even autumn can kill.*

"And the beasts. That's more danger than I've ever seen here. This Place has changed," Wolfson goes on. "My whole life, it's never been like this. But it is now. And no one knows why."

They reach the top of the hill that will lead them back down to the Salt River, and from here they can see the lights of the town.

"I'm going to tell you what the fountain told me," Wolfson says abruptly, stopping on the path. He stares at the ground between Henry and Ndidi.

"Okay," Ndidi says softly when he doesn't speak for a while.

"It said, *Your mother never loved you.*"

Henry's heart feels like it's sinking into the dirt under their feet. Wolfson goes on staring at it. Henry looks at Ndidi, but her eyes, shiny with tears, are fixed on Wolfson.

"You don't have to say anything," he says. "Please don't. I just felt like...I should say it. I've been thinking a lot about her and what I remember. I remember...the way she was. But I don't even remember my real name."

227

What the fountain whispered to Henry was bad enough, but this? The kind of thing that would sting from the mean kid at school. But the truth of it rising up from a bubble, from the bottom of the world?

"There's no way that's true," Henry says. "That fountain wasn't even a fountain."

Ndidi stares at her, and Wolfson shakes his head.

"No, it is true," he says. "I feel it."

"No," Henry insists. "I'm telling you it's not true."

Because if what Wolfson was told isn't true, maybe what she was told isn't either.

"Henry, you're not—" Ndidi starts, but she's interrupted.

Screaming.

The sound of it rises up from below.

Wolfson's head jolts up from where it was hanging low. All three of them stare toward the town. They can't see people, only the torches that they carry, running back and forth, scattering.

"Oh no," Wolfson says. And before they can say a word, about his mother or about the night, he's gone, plunging through the tall grass toward town.

CHAPTER 21

t's Jamila," a man with a white beard calls when he sees Wolfson. It doesn't matter that Wolfson is a child—the adults outside the hostel all turn to him when they see that he's arrived. "It chased her. Her arm..."

Wolfson's parents appear at the edge of the light, both panting.

We chased it, his mother says. *But it disappeared.*

Like smoke, his father adds.

"What disappeared?" Ndidi says. Between the dark and people shouting, the torn tents and baskets of spilled fruit, everything feels like chaos. Her eyes brim with tears. Henry's heart is hammering, but she never cries when she's scared. Her muscles flex. Her father always called her an "inside girl," she thinks, but no one ever tagged her out in kickball because when Henry gets nervous she runs so fast the wind can't catch her. She's on the verge of running now.

"A beast," she says. She knows.

The man with the white beard nods.

"It showed up as soon as the suns sank," he says, wringing his hands. "Went into the children's hostel. Inside! She must have surprised it. It was in your room, Ndidi! Jamila was taking cookies door-to-door, and she found it there. It bit her, and then Yasmin was there with candles and scared it away."

"Is Jamila okay?" Ndidi cries, her voice begging. "It bit her. Is she all right?"

"I don't know," the man says. "I don't think so. She is asleep. The white is spreading up her arm. White, like the beasts."

"Like someone has painted her," another man says. "I can see it swirling under her skin. Spreading up just a hair, so slow you don't notice."

"What does it mean?" Henry asks. It feels like being back in the snow. Her teeth chatter. *Adrenaline*, she knows her father would say.

"We don't know. And we can't find Angie anywhere."

"Let's go check on Jamila first. Are all the children inside?" Wolfson asks.

No one seems to notice that Wolfson is a child himself.

Everyone nods, and Ndidi moves off to help the people whose market tents got messed up. Already, the suns are coming up again. Night and day dodging in and out of sight.

"It makes no sense," people say, glancing up at the sky in fear. "No moon, and the night so short. Not a night at all. How do you dream without night?"

Henry doesn't want to sleep. There's an itch in her mind, and Ndidi is bent down scooping up spilled beads, always helping. It doesn't seem to have sunk in that the beast was in her room. Not just Ndidi's—Henry's.

Henry passes the groups of people who linger outside the hostel, all of them peering down. The beast left paw prints through the kitchen and up the stairs. Paw prints on the ramps too—the beast had roamed. Henry follows the prints—silver tiger paws the size of dinner plates. They're beginning to fade in places, but not so pale that she can't follow the beast's trail down the hall to where she and Ndidi sleep.

Silver tracks through the doorway, right to the edge of Henry's bed.

The feeling starts in her stomach, then travels up to her throat. Icy claw, gripping her breath. She reaches for her pillow and lifts its edge. At first she thinks it's gone. But she lifts a little more and finds it there waiting, a faint silver sparkle in the strange dawn outside.

The necklace.

Henry's feet carry her back downstairs and out the door. No one notices when she leaves the market, where all the chaos is still settling. From one of the windows of the hostel, she can hear some of the smaller children crying. It's almost enough to make her go back, but she can't. Everyone is worried about Jamila, but the only thing Henry can think of is what the fountain whispered in her ear: *Your father is a thief.*

She presses her hand to the lump of the necklace under her shirt. She can smell the icy breath of the beasts when she blinks for too long. But while her eyes are closed, her mind feels like a collage, little shreds coming together: the beasts, her father, and this necklace. *Your father is a thief.* Is this what he stole? The necklace isn't the only lump. Henry feels the one in her throat—it showed up even before the fountain. She feels full of questions she never asks. She remembers what the bees said: *stepping off the map.* Maybe it is time to step off a little more.

Away from town without being noticed, she follows her feet to the path she's taken only once. But she knows the way. To be a thief, one must steal something, and all the some-things Henry knows of in this world are in one place.

Christopher's.

CHAPTER 22

enry finds him in the center of the junkyard, where his desk is. The plants that she'd noticed on the ceiling are at floor level now: They're on a huge platform that's attached to a system of pulleys, and Christopher has wheeled the whole thing down. He has his back to her, humming and pruning. He's not a giant today, not yet. But Henry knows, like everything else in This Place, how quickly this can change.

"What did your boss send me today?" he calls without turning to face her. "Tell her I have enough hairpins."

"She didn't send anything," Henry says. "I . . . I sent myself. I'm here alone."

The humming stops abruptly, and so does the motion of his hands through the leaves of a giant fern.

"What do you want?"

She wants the question to be an arrow. *Did my father steal this necklace from you?* But she mentioned a necklace before, and Christopher said nothing about a theft. She considers showing him the necklace, but it occurs to her that he may not yet realize it's gone. What if he sees it now and is angry at Henry instead? He could force her to give it back. Although, she isn't sure she wants it anymore. When she looks at it, she sees saliva dripping from fangs.

"*Yes?*" he says, looking a little larger now.

"Did you hear about the beasts?" she blurts. "Going into town?"

His hands drift down to his sides.

"No," he says. "I didn't."

"They chased me again," Henry says. "The other night. I found the Small Part. Tonight the beasts came and bit a girl. Jamila."

Silence.

"What happens to someone if they die in This Place?" she asks.

The frown moves up to his eyes, becoming a scowl. "I'll let you know when I find out."

"What?"

He turns away. "What do you need? More wood? Screws?"

"Where do the beasts come from?" she asks, ignoring him.

"I don't know."

He won't look at her, and for a moment she wonders if the beasts belong to him somehow. Everyone is afraid of him, and he lives separate from everyone. Then again, so does Emma.

"Do they have anything to do with Emma?" she asks. "The lonely woman?"

"Two-Time Emma," he says, shaking his head. "No, she has her own monsters."

"She does?"

He snorts. "Not that kind. They're not yours to face. They're hers. And that's why she's still here. Me too. And Angie."

"Are the beasts...are the beasts yours?"

He shoots her a look as he removes his gardening gloves. "Good question. But no."

She believes him and relaxes. She doesn't know if that's smart or not.

"Where are your friends?" he asks.

"In town. I came by myself today."

"With beasts on the run?" he says. His frown is disapproving now. "Surely your father would have taught you better."

Henry's heart skips a beat.

"That's why I'm here."

"What's why?"

"To ask you about my dad."

"What about him?"

"Did my dad...did he...did he steal from you?" she finally says. It feels sour to say. Like she has taken a side against her father just by asking.

"Nobody can steal from me," Christopher says.

"His compass—the one I asked you about—"

"Is still here with me."

"Did you take it from him? Or did you trade?"

He scowls. "I only trade. And I resent the implication."

"Remember the necklace I told you about? Is that what he traded for?"

"Let me see it."

She's still reluctant. Christopher is like a vault, sealed tight. He gives nothing away. She reaches for the chain at her neck and pulls the pendant out of her shirt.

He studies it silently, then raises his eyes to Henry. His expression is stone.

"Why are you asking?" he says. "I'm not trading you the compass. Not for that."

"Does that mean this is what he traded you for?" Henry demands.

"Why does it matter?" he snaps. "All this hounding. You want to know what your father did while he was here, go home and ask him."

236

"I'm trying!"

"No, you're not!" Her head has to tilt far back to see him now—he's growing large again. Angie said when someone felt small, they ended up in the Small Part. Whatever Christopher is feeling, it isn't small. His voice booms: "Something is keeping you here. And worse than these other fools, you know exactly what it is. You're here because you want to be— you know that this is a searching place, and you're spending time nosing around in someone else's looking."

He hauls on the rope, sending the garden on the platform back toward the ceiling. He ties it off, and there it stays, as if floating.

"It's all the same flower," Henry says, surprised. She looks around. She doesn't know why she didn't notice it before— soft purple coloring the room. *Angie's flowers?* "Why do you like them so much?"

He looks at her as if she struck him.

"Another night," he says, pointing at the window, the suns setting yet again. She can't keep up. "And I won't let you leave here alone with the beasts about. I'll show you to a room."

"I don't want to sleep here."

"You don't have a choice. You can't go out there in the dark. This Place isn't as gentle as it used to be."

He's not wrong. And Christopher may not be friendly, but she'd rather be around him than the beasts. She tries to picture the bite that the girl named Jamila has on her arm. White tendrils spreading through her skin. Henry shudders.

"Follow me," Christopher says.

She does, but now she can't stop seeing the flowers.

"The purple," she says, and she dares to ask the question out loud. "Aren't they the same ones Angie keeps around her stall in the market? They're the same color."

He wheels on her in the small hallway. The look on his face makes her flinch.

"No. More. Questions." His voice takes up all the space that his body doesn't. He storms down the hall, the bigness of his shoulders jolting some of the things he's collected off their shelves. A trail of things behind him like space junk after a rocket.

"Why do you have such a problem with questions?" Henry cries, surprising herself. "You said This Place is for searching— isn't that what questions are?"

"Exactly," he shouts over his shoulder. "Something I have no wish to do."

"Then how will you ever leave?!"

"I won't!" he thunders. "I will not!"

He yanks open a door and stands beside it, pointing her inside.

"Sleep," he says.

"Tell me about the necklace," she demands. "You have

everything here. All this stuff. All these things you know. And you won't give any of it away. For no reason!"

He glares down the hall, not looking at her, silent.

"I'll give you back the necklace—for free—if you tell me about my dad. Anything! Just tell me *something*."

"I don't want it," he says. Then they're eye to eye, almost instantaneously. She hadn't even noticed him shrink.

"Christopher, please. I—"

"You what?" he says.

"I need to know," she says finally. "About him."

"Ask him," he says. "I don't want to hear any more about daughters and their fathers."

When he moves away down the hall, surrounded by everything he has collected, it's like a wind is chasing him.

"Christopher, please!" she yells. "His compass is here! Where did he go without it?"

He stops short. She almost thinks he'll turn, but he doesn't.

"None of it matters. He needed more than a compass or a necklace to go up the witch's mountain."

"Up the mountain? My father went up the mountain?"

He shoots the barest of glances over his shoulder just before he turns the corner.

"I don't know—did he? You should know the man better than I."

Then he's gone, and Henry is alone with the smell of

239

239

purple flowers. Her head feels like it's spinning. Christopher didn't just say *the mountain*. He said the *witch's* mountain. Does that mean the witch is actually real? If her father went up there...did he meet her? Henry pulls the map from her father's pack.

She was right—the floating river isn't there. She takes up a little pencil that she found at the dormitory, studying where she walked. Her father's positioning of the fountain was a little off, she realizes. Too close to the Pepper Sea. She draws a circle around it, and an arrow, then draws the river. It looks like a noodle with waves inside.

Then she stares at the mountain, the X her father drew just above.

The map only makes her more restless. She keeps thinking about what the bees said. This is all on her father's map— but what would she find if she stepped off?

CHAPTER 23

She stays in the room Christopher showed her to—filled entirely with hairpins—for only an hour before slipping out and wandering the halls of the junkyard. Henry has a searching feeling. Even if she doesn't know what she's looking for. There's a section for everything—it makes her think of her grandmother's sewing room. Yarn here, needles there. Everything in its place. Henry ends up back in the room where she found her father's compass. She expects to find it there, Christopher having returned it to its spot. But it's still gone. Henry feels a strange relief. Would she have taken it this time? There are other compasses, and she touches them.

Something moves in the corner of her eye. She jumps. *The beast.*

But it's not the beast. It's Christopher.

"No questions," he says. "But I'll show you something."

She follows him, twisting and turning through the junk-yard. They pass rooms and rooms of things. Henry thinks suddenly of Uncle Cecil. *It's what people do*, he said. *They either surround themselves with memories like a pack rat, or they roam looking for something more.* These aren't Christopher's memories. But it does feel like a pack rat's burrow. Safe with all the things. Cushioned from the outside.

"Here," Christopher says. He pauses at the door to a room off the main corridor. Henry peeks in.

It's filled with shoes. Some are bowling shoes. Golf shoes. High heels. Work boots. Sneakers. House slippers. Baby shoes.

Her eyes land on a pair of hiking boots at the same moment Christopher says: "Recognize any?"

She rushes to the wall where they sit and reaches out, but then pulls back cautiously.

"Can I?"

He shrugs in answer.

She picks up the boots. They were her father's. His casual pair—not what he wore for serious adventures, but a comfortable pair that one of the sponsorship companies had sent him. Not waterproof. Basic boots.

"Your father needed something more serious for the climb,

I think," Christopher says. He won't say anything more. She knows he's talking about her father's climb of the mountain.

She hugs the boots like they're her father himself. He traded them, then. The same way he traded the compass. When he was packing for a trip once, he showed Henry how he saved space in his bag by stuffing clean socks inside shoes. She reaches inside one of the boots. Empty. She reaches in the other.

She feels paper.

It's another note, written on the same small paper as the one Emma was saving. Ragged at one edge from being ripped from his tiny notebook. This time it's not crumpled, but folded carefully.

> Dear Reader,
>
> Don't waste this opportunity. What lies behind you is nothing compared with what lies before you. No one knows how this place works—the truth is yours to shape as you see fit. Life is the greatest adventure.

She hears it in his voice. It's the kind of thing he would caption his videos with on Instagram. People loved her father.

He made them feel so hopeful and excited. *So inspirational,* people would comment. Henry's stomach feels sour. She thinks it's silly to have wished the note was addressed to her. Why would he ever think she would end up here, walking the same steps he had walked?

She thinks about the nail, the bees, running away to Christopher's to try to fix things. *Maybe,* she thinks, *I'm walking my own path.*

Henry's fingers flicker.

She freezes. Stares at the note. Was it the light shining down on the paper? Or did she…?

"Your father and I had a lot in common," Christopher says. Henry jumps. She almost forgot he was there.

"Did he talk about me?"

She's not exactly sure how the question escaped from her mouth. If the nurses had been right about an alien abduction, Henry would have asked the aliens too. *Did he talk about me? Did he think about me? Did he want to come home?* The thing about asking questions is the answers. Henry is waiting for his.

It feels like a very long silence. She shoves the note into her pocket, fighting back tears.

"I knew your name from your father," he says eventually. "He didn't talk about his life much. But when he did, it was *I need to take this back to show Henry.* Little things. Sea glass. A tiny bone."

"A piece of hive."

"Yes."

"He doesn't bring those things for me," she says. She's surprised by how angry she sounds. "He brings them back for his shelves. To show everyone else all the places he's been. The things he's seen."

Christopher doesn't look at her.

"I was a parent once. It's very easy to get confused."

"About what?"

"About what is for your child, and what is for yourself."

"My dad was in This Place, and it was all for him," she says. Her voice sounds loud in the room full of shoes. "He didn't care about coming home. All he cared about was seeing it all for the map."

"Your dad was in This Place?"

It's not Christopher's voice; it's Ndidi's. Christopher has been shrinking, and now he's small enough to leave space in the doorway around him. Wolfson and Ndidi are there, Angie just behind them. They all wear different frowns.

"Christopher," Angie says.

"Angie."

"What map?" Ndidi says.

"Her father was the mapmaker," Wolfson says. His face has the serene wolf look of his parents. "It was before you came, Ndidi. A man was here that thought he was discovering This Place."

"He was," Henry says.

"How can you discover what is already full of people?" Ndidi says.

"No, discovering it for himself."

"That's not what discovering means," Wolfson says quietly.

"He was here?" Ndidi says. Her frown is so confused it makes Henry's heart sink. "He was here and went home?"

And then the question Henry dreaded most:

"Why didn't you tell us?"

"Christopher, we need your help," Angie says. She steps around Wolfson and Ndidi. "A girl was hurt."

"What help can I give?" he says bitterly.

"Whatever you're able to," she says evenly. "I'm going to see the Woman at the Top of the World."

"The witch?" he says, almost laughing.

"The witch?" Henry repeats.

"Yes. She will know what to do," Angie says. "But there is no time to climb the mountain. The girl that was bitten is getting worse. I need to take the balloon."

Angie and Christopher stare at each other in a strange way, and yesterday Henry might have wondered why. Today,

246

she sees more. She sees the purple flowers planted in every hanging garden of the junkyard. She sees the piles of color-coordinated clothes that remind her of when her parents would fold laundry together on Sundays. She sees the vases of spoons and forks, organized and waiting. There is something that connects Angie and Christopher. Henry doesn't know what it is. But she sees it.

He turns away.

"Take whatever you need," he says.

"That's not good enough, Christopher," Angie says. Her voice catches at him like a hook.

"Nothing is."

He storms out and down the hall, growing larger and larger.

"You're the only one she'll give it to," Angie calls after him. "But only if you ask. You have to ask."

"What are they talking about?" Henry says.

"They're talking about Emma," Wolfson says softly.

"Emma?" she says, surprised. "What about Emma?"

"I think ... I think they came here together. Angie. Christopher. Emma."

Christopher has stopped in the middle of the hall, but he doesn't turn to look at Angie.

"Emma won't speak to me, Angie," he says.

"You have to try. You're her father. I know this is hard, but you have to try."

Christopher is silent. He doesn't move. Angie's face is streaked with tears—Wolfson notices at the same time Henry does, and he breaks away, moving toward Christopher.

"If you would just come out!" Wolfson cries. "Hiding in this place helps nothing!"

"*Everyone* in This Place is hiding," Christopher shouts, and finally he turns back. "And does it matter? It finds you! The sadness finds you!"

"So come out!" Wolfson demands. Henry has never seen him look more like his parents than he does now: his whole body stiff, his eyes intense. "Can't you see it's making her sad? She's trying to help you!"

"She's not your mother, child," Christopher says. "She may act like a mother, but she's not yours."

Henry had still been clutching her father's boots—she doesn't realize she's thrown one until it's already out of her hand and striking Christopher in the chest. Now it bounces onto the floor.

"Watch your mouth!" she shouts. "You just watch your mouth! Don't say that to him!"

It's something her mother says, although not anymore. She said it a lot when Henry's father first disappeared. She kept insisting he would return, and Henry would say, *But it's been eight days, ten days, twelve days.* And Henry's mother would tell her to watch her mouth. And eventually she did, going in the bathroom and watching herself say, *But he's been gone twenty-six days.* It didn't make her not say the words. It just made her say them silently.

Everyone is silent. Christopher is not a giant anymore.

"Brave like your father," he says. "And foolish too."

Henry clutches the other boot, the one that had contained her father's note.

"We'll need rope," Christopher says quietly. "You brought the wagon?"

"Yes," Angie answers.

"I'll meet you outside."

Eunice and Eustace are waiting when Henry and the others step out. The suns are rising again, for however long this day decides to be. Ndidi and Wolfson huddle by the wagon. They study Henry when she joins them.

"I want to see the map," Ndidi says. She radiates a coldness that makes Henry feel small.

Henry pulls it from her pack. The three of them study it, unfolded.

"The tree," Wolfson says. "With the bees. You wanted to climb it because it was on his map?"

"I guess so."

Ndidi shakes her head. Henry has never disappointed a friend before. Not like this.

"Why didn't you tell us?" Ndidi says. "Why keep it a secret?"

She remembers what Ndidi said in the kitchen the morning Javier found his way: No one likes to repeat their own mistakes. Henry certainly does not want to repeat this one. But even with the truth about her father out in the open, some truths are still too hard to say. Her father's notes left in This Place, and Henry in none of them.

Christopher emerges from the junkyard, his arms full. Into the wagon go rope and cable. A large hook, so big and heavy it jolts the wagon when he puts it inside.

"You know how to find her?" he asks Angie.

"Yes, I was with her when the girl was bitten."

"That's where you were?" Wolfson says. "With Emma?"

"Not now," Angie says gently. "For now, let's go. All of us."

CHAPTER 24

The wagon stops in a meadow Henry doesn't recognize. They veered off the path at Angie's direction, onto flat dirt that eventually gave way to clover and purple flowers. Acres of them. They blossom on and on.

"She won't speak to me, Angie," Christopher says quietly.

"She will."

"I've looked for her before. She never lets me find her."

Henry slowly begins to understand. The pieces are like a collage in her mind—little things coming together.

"She's your daughter," Henry says. "Emma?"

Angie looks at her like she wishes she hadn't spoken, but Henry thinks she's been quiet enough for long enough. Christopher answers.

"We got lost together," he says. "Then she was gone for a while. But she must still be missing something. Because she's here again."

"In the Small Part," Henry says. "Waiting for you."

"No," he says doubtfully. But there's a crack in the doubt. "Not for me."

"Go to her, Christopher," Angie says. "We had only just begun to know each other when we arrived. What she needs I can't give. You can."

"What if she won't speak to me?" he says.

"But what if she will?" Ndidi says.

When he shrinks into the Small Part, Ndidi and Henry and Wolfson watch him go. Angie keeps her eyes on the donkeys, standing between them, stroking their necks.

"Is he going to be okay?" Wolfson says. "I wish I could help him."

"It's not a child's job to help an adult," Angie says.

"Why is it yours?" Wolfson says.

"Because I love him," Angie says simply. "And we want what's best for people we love. Even if we don't always go about it the right way."

"Did you see that?" Ndidi says, a little shrill.

Henry and Wolfson look at her, alarmed, but Ndidi is looking at her hands.

"I . . . for a second I thought I . . . never mind. Sorry. I imagined it."

Angie turns to look off toward the Pepper Sea. She's thinking of Jamila, of the pale white tendrils snaking up her arm.

"It's not our job to help Christopher, but we can help
Jamila," she says quietly.

"By going to the witch?" Henry says. "I thought there was
no such thing?"

"There isn't," Angie says firmly. "Because she is not a
witch."

"You never told me about her," Wolfson says, looking at
the dirt.

"I've only met her once," she answers. "But right now I
need you to go back to town. Do you understand? I will wait
here for Christopher. But you go back to town. I need you to
prepare supplies. Can you do that for me? Gather the things
I'll need for the trip up the mountain? In case . . ."

She trails off.

"In case?" Ndidi says.

"In case I am wrong about Emma."

"What does Emma have that we need?" Henry asks, trying to keep up.

"Gas," Angie says. "For the hot-air balloon."

Henry thinks back to the small house, its corners and its

messy bed. There in the corner of the kitchen, the big cylinder. She thought it was helium.

"I saw it," Henry says. "When I was there. The tank."

"Yes." Angie nods. "I'll need it for the balloon to take me up the mountain. But if she won't give it to us, then I'll have to climb, which will take much longer. I'll need supplies."

"I'm going with you," Wolfson says.

"Wolfson..."

"You're not going alone," he says stubbornly.

"Someone needs to stay with the town," she says. "To keep an eye on everyone."

"Someone else..."

"No one else knows everything I know the way you do," Angie tells him gently. "I know you'd prefer not to deal with new people, but—"

"Angie, you should stay," Henry interrupts.

They all look at her. Her cheeks burn.

"Sorry, but...you should stay. What if the beasts come back? Wolfson can't protect everyone alone."

"Neither can Angie!" Wolfson cries.

"I'll go with him," Henry says, ignoring him. "Up the mountain. So he won't be by himself."

"It's too dangerous," Angie says, shaking her head.

"It's *all* dangerous," Wolfson cries. "You can't do it all by yourself."

"Let me think about this," Angie says gently. "For now, can you go to town? While there's light? Can you do that for me?"

She places her hand on Wolfson's back. It makes Henry's chest tight. Wolfson just nods, but she can almost hear his heart saying *mother*.

CHAPTER 25

enry saw the balloon, the same way she saw the many other things stranded in This Place. The boats along the beach, the cluster of cars close to Christopher's junkyard. The balloon is red and blue and yellow, and it's draped over the limb of one of the thick trees outside the market.

"So if Emma gives us the tank," Ndidi says, "the balloon will carry Angie up the mountain?"

"Carry *me* up the mountain," Wolfson says. "Henry is right. Angie needs to stay here. To look after everything and to be here if new people show up."

"Wolfson, are you sure o? This is a witch we're talking about."

"Angie says she's not a witch."

"Angie has only met her once!"

"That's more than anybody else."

Ndidi and Henry have to jog to keep up with him as he angles toward the hostel.

"Is she at the very top?" Henry pants. "That's what Angie called her, right? The Woman at the Top of the World."

"Yes, the very top, she said."

"Why don't you just look at your map?" Ndidi says.

The sharpness of Ndidi's voice makes Henry slow down. Wolfson too. He glances between them.

"Say it," he says. "What are we talking about?"

"Henry doesn't want to help Jamila. She just wants to explore her father's map."

"That's not true," Henry says.

"It is," Ndidi says. "That's why you didn't tell us. You've been lying since you got here o. Haven't you?"

"No."

"Another lie!" Ndidi says. She sounds more and more upset. "How do I know? Because the Fountain of Truth told me."

Wolfson frowns.

"What are you saying, Ndidi?"

Ndidi crosses her arms.

"Henry said she wanted to go to the Fountain of Truth to see if it would show her a way to go home. That's what you said, Henry. But what did the fountain tell me?"

"What did it say?" Henry says.

Ndidi's eyes fill with tears.

"It doesn't matter. It proves you're a liar."

"We don't have time for this right now," Wolfson says quietly. "Maybe later."

He turns and continues moving toward the hostel, leaving Henry and Ndidi alone. Henry wishes she could speak. How to say *I lied, but I'm not a liar*? Is there a difference?

The market is empty, everyone worried about the strange swooping night and when it might fall. If the beasts need the night to come, Henry thinks they are getting more and more opportunities. She and Ndidi move silently across the ground, following Wolfson to the hostel. The only other things moving are the bats, plunging down from the hostel roof to the big tree at the center of the market. They haven't bothered anyone—just swooped back and forth. The quiet makes This Place feel wrong—everyone going about their business was the only thing that kept it all from feeling haunted. Now the sad waiting feeling that always seems to be crouched at the edge of the world dives down like the bats.

In the kitchen of the hostel, Ndidi and Henry stand far apart, watching Wolfson.

"I know we don't actually need food," he says. "But I'm... hungry?" He looks worried. "I haven't felt it like this since... well, in a long time."

"Do you think it means something else is changing?" Ndidi says. "What if This Place is falling apart? What happens to all the people here if it does? What if...?"

She doesn't finish her sentence, but Henry knows what she was going to say: *What if it means we all never go home? That our families miss us forever?*

"What if it means everyone goes home?" Wolfson says, so softly Henry almost doesn't hear.

"Best-case scenario," Henry says.

He looks up, right into her eyes.

"Not for me."

They're all silent while he stuffs bags. He reaches into drawers for tools as well as food.

"What else do we need?" Henry says, opening cupboards.

"You don't need to go," he says.

"Yes, I do. Did you see Angie's face when I said it? She'll feel better about you going if someone goes with you. And..." She pauses. It's hard to get these words out. "Yes, I want to go because my dad went up there. But that's why you should let me come. I have the map."

"He doesn't need a map to know where the top of a mountain is," Ndidi says coldly.

"Still," Henry says.

"Quiet," Wolfson says, holding up his hand. His eyes are wide. "I hear the wagon."

He grabs the packs, and the three of them rush outside into the strange quiet. He was right: The wagon appears an inch at a time over a rise in the land. Eustace and Eunice, Angie walking beside them. Then, behind the wagon, two figures.

Christopher, tall. And small, next to him, Emma.

"They did it," Wolfson whispers.

In the back of the wagon Henry can make out the shape of the tank. The donkeys take short, quick steps, the whole group rattling closer.

"We need to get the balloon," Wolfson says, dropping the things he'd packed.

"But shouldn't we ask—" Henry starts, but Ndidi is already running after him, so Henry takes one more look at Christopher walking beside his daughter, and she runs after them.

The balloon inflates slowly, and they all watch in silence. Henry steals looks at Christopher, who stands so close to Emma he could touch her, but doesn't.

"I have an idea," Angie said when Wolfson, Henry, and Ndidi came dragging the balloon toward the market. "Bring it to the rope."

Henry remembers the rope from her first day in This Place— it's still there, bolted to the ground beside the metal wheel.

"The other end goes straight to the mountain," Angie says.

"How do you know?" says Wolfson. He shields his eyes from the suns, peering off into the sky after the rope.

"Because I found it when I was up there. Staked to another metal bolt, deep in the rock."

"I didn't know you actually went up there," Wolfson says, eyes wide.

"Before you came," she says, smiling. Then she moves closer to him and bends so their eyes meet. "You understand that I wouldn't let you do this under any other circumstances? Not for fun, not for anything?"

He says nothing.

"The Woman at the Top of the World doesn't interfere down here," she says. "But you've been here longer than almost anyone else. I think she will do this for us."

Wolfson's eyes fill with tears. *Us* with Angie is a thing he needs to hear.

"You will be careful," Angie says firmly. "You will be careful, and you will be quick, and you will come back here. Do you understand?"

He nods once, decisively. When Angie hugs him, Henry has nowhere to look. Christopher and Emma. Angie and Wolfson. Like Ndidi, she looks at the ground until Eustace and Eunice begin to paw the dirt and Angie lets go.

"Let's get this done," she says, and straightens.

Angie describes the plan. The hot-air balloon is attached to the rope using cable from Christopher's yard. When the gas is turned on, the balloon will rise, but Wolfson will not have to steer. Tethered to the rope, the balloon will make its way up the mountain to the end of the rope.

"Was there a person in it?" Henry asks, watching the shape of the balloon high up on the mountain. "When it got here?"

"Us," Emma says. She looks at Christopher. "It was ours."

Inside the basket, she shows Wolfson how to turn off the gas.

"Turn it off, and then get out. We'll worry about how to get it down later."

The balloon is on a leash, Eustace says. *Like we used to be.*

The two donkeys chuckle, but their laughter has a bitter sound. Henry thinks that if she were them, she would never want to find her way—back to humans they can't talk to and bits in their mouths. Maybe their place is here, like Wolfson. Maybe they intend to stay.

"Plan for when we get up there?" Ndidi says, glancing at Wolfson.

"We?" he says.

"Sha, you didn't think I'm staying here? Please. So, plan?"

"She lives at the very top," he says, shrugging. "The balloon will get us close. We'll walk the rest of the way. You really don't have to come."

"Hush," Ndidi says.

The basket attached to the balloon is the size of a Jacuzzi. Rather than clunking down onto the ground, it hovers about an inch over it. The gas makes a soft shushing sound.

"Ready?" Wolfson says, swinging the bags of food into the basket.

He's reaching for the sack at Ndidi's feet when the first beast slams into him.

Ndidi's scream rips through the air, and the donkeys' sounds of terror make Henry's blood freeze. Wolfson manages to roll out from under the white beast, but it's already turned away from him anyway, setting its sights on Henry and Ndidi.

"Stay away," Ndidi cries. "Back!"

Henry grabs her and they run, trying to put the basket between them and the beast. It leaps over the bolt in the ground, clambering over Eunice, who brays in pain and fear. The beast's shaggy white limbs get tangled in the rope. Wolfson springs to Eunice's aid, his hands struggling to free both animals from the harnesses so they can run. Angie and Christopher wrestle with a second beast. Christopher has it by the tail, Angie scrabbling backward on the ground. Emma is nowhere in sight.

"Go!" Angie shouts. "Into the basket!"

Henry tries, but the basket is tall. She and Ndidi scramble, feet sliding against the smooth wicker. Wolfson has climbed in through the door on the other side and appears over the top, reaching down to help drag them up and inside. He cranks the gas when the beast leaps, the arc of it landing right over the edge of the basket, its teeth like moonstone, sparkling so bright in Henry's eyes she swears they glow.

On the floor of the basket, her hands find a sandbag. She stands quickly, hefting it with her, then uses all her strength to swing it against the beast's face. Its claws scrabble at the wicker, tearing it and leaving splinters, but it falls just as the balloon lifts from the ground. There's a crank at the edge of the basket, and Wolfson turns it frantically, the balloon lifting higher and faster. The whole basket jolts and sways as the other beast leaps, clawing at its bottom. It sends them careening sideways, swinging like a pendulum. One of the sacks of supplies topples out, and from this angle Henry sees the two beasts pounce on it, thinking it was one of them. She sees Angie pulling Emma into the hostel as Christopher closes them all safely inside. Henry lets out a ragged sigh.

They may be beasts, but they can't fly.

The balloon is well into the air now, moving smoothly along the track of the rope that will lead them to the mountain.

"Are you okay?" Ndidi asks Wolfson. His shirt is streaked with red.

"It's not mine," he says, still breathing hard. "Eunice's. I . . . I hope she'll be okay."

"She will be," Ndidi says.

"And Angie . . ."

"She will be," Henry echoes. "They're in the hostel. They're okay."

Ndidi looks at Henry with a face she can't read, but something about it looks accusing. Like to her, this is all Henry's fault. A feeling is growing inside Henry, a feeling like something heavy around her neck. A feeling that says Ndidi might be right.

CHAPTER 26

When the balloon reaches the end of its track, at first
Henry thinks they're so high they've found snow. The
place where they land is covered in a coat of sparkling
white. It blankets the ground, the trees, the rocky outcrops that
build toward the mountaintop. It's not until Wolfson jumps
out of the basket that they realize it's not snow at all.

"Butterflies," Ndidi breathes in wonder. Wolfson's pres-
ence on the ground sends the millions of them into the air.
Everything is thick with butterflies. They billow and rise,
beautiful but eerie too. Like pieces of a ghost trying to find
their way back together again. Henry and Ndidi jump out of
the basket after Wolfson, and when the butterflies resettle, it's
only in the trees. The rocky ground is clear now, and Henry's

glad not to worry about stepping on them. With the butterflies gone, she also sees something their bodies disguised.

A campsite.

"Let's see if there's anything we can use," Wolfson says. "We lost one of the sacks."

"We need to make a fire," Ndidi says. "Night can come at any time now with things so strange. And if the beasts find us, we need to be prepared."

"I know how," Henry says, stepping toward the fire pit. "I can do it fast depending on what's around here."

This is a thing she does well. Her father taught her to make a fire early on. *Inside girl or not*, he said, *this isn't about camping. It's about survival. You get lost, you lose power, you need to figure out how to stay warm. Hypothermia can set in faster than you think.*

It's not cold right now. But it's not night right now either. Like hypothermia, Henry knows how fast things can change in This Place.

And then she sees the backpack.

She recognizes it from an older YouTube video. One of her father's many gifts from sponsors, except this was one he actually liked. Big and yellow, it replaced his old brown pack almost immediately, and he used nothing else. She and her mother looked everywhere for that pack with the search parties. Hard to miss something that color. But they never found it either. Now she knows why.

"Someone left their bag," Ndidi says, coming up behind her. "What's in it?"

Henry almost lies. Telling the truth, after all, is a reminder of the lies she's already told. But there's blood on Wolfson's shirt. This is a time for truth.

"That's . . . that's my dad's backpack."

Ndidi is silent for a moment before she speaks. "Then I guess you're doing a good job following his map."

"What's in the bag?" Wolfson says.

She could tell them what had been in it before This Place—she knows Dad's packing list by heart. But she can't guess about what is left now. The compass is down in Christopher's junkyard, waiting to be traded for. Her heart sinks as she goes to the pack, digging through.

"Starter tinder. Stormproof matches. Emergency tent. Bear spray. We can use that on the beasts for sure."

"Bear spray," Ndidi repeated, raising her eyebrow. "What is that? You know it?"

"Yeah, sure," she says. "My dad is . . . well, he was an explorer." She shoots a look at Wolfson. "Which is not the same thing as a discoverer."

"Funny thing for an explorer to end up in a place like This Place," Ndidi says. She doesn't sound as mean now.

"Yeah, funny," Henry says bitterly. "So funny he didn't want to come home."

Ndidi looks at her sharply. "What do you mean?"

"I don't know. Nothing."

"Doing it again," Wolfson calls without looking up.

But then Henry's fingers find one last thing at the bottom of the pack. Hard, rectangular. The edge of paper. She knows before she pulls it out that it's her father's notebook.

It's almost empty, the inside of it filled with the ragged margin from tearing sheets out. Some of them, she knows, are pinned to his map in the basement at home—little notes to himself that he'd jotted down when out on an adventure. Something to add to his next video, or a place he should visit, a sponsor to email. And some of them, she knows, are scattered all over This Place. Two at least, which she had found. What if she stayed in This Place and turned over every single stone, looking for his handwriting? Would she have the answers to all her questions? What even are they?

All the pages left in the notebook are blank except one.

Should I call Henrietta "Henry"?

She can't take her eyes off the words. Somewhere between the junkyard and this spot on the mountain, her father had remembered she existed.

"Why are you crying?" Ndidi says, sounding worried. "What's wrong?"

"I just..."

Her lip trembles. Then her hands too.

"What's the matter, Henry?"

"I...can I tell you what the fountain told me?"

Ndidi looks surprised. Maybe she had been expecting
more lies. Wolfson's face is as placid as ever, but he watches
Henry carefully.

"What did it tell you?" Ndidi says softly.

"It said...it said...my father is a thief."

Ndidi gasps. Wolfson frowns.

"A thief?" Ndidi says. "A thief of what?"

"Of everything," Henry says.

"The fountain said that?"

"No," Henry cries. "*I* said that."

"What did he...?"

"This," Henry says, snatching at her shirt. "Do you see this
necklace? I...I have a bad feeling that..."

The words catch in her throat. She remembers how adults
make a shelter with their words, to shield her. She wants to
make a shelter with hers now, to shield the two of them. But
Wolfson is bleeding. This is not a time for lies.

"I have a bad feeling about this necklace," she says, hanging her head. "I...thought he traded for it at first. But..."

"Maybe the fountain meant the beehive," Wolfson says.
"He stole that too."

"What?" Henry cries, shocked. "No, that's not..."

But then she thinks of how pleased the bees were to have it back. *Yes, this is ours.* And Emma's nail. The one that, once returned, fixed her weather vane.

"He takes things," Henry says quietly. "I never thought that made him a thief."

"Just like you didn't know telling lies makes you a liar?" Ndidi says. She sounds mean again, but she also sounds like she wants to cry.

"What about you?" Henry snaps, brushing away her tears. "You didn't even want to say what the fountain said. Why not? You said it proved I was a liar, but what did it say about *you?*"

"It wasn't just about me!" Ndidi cries. "It was about..."

She stops, her eyes shining. They dart at Wolfson.

"Say it," he says softly.

Ndidi sniffs. "All of us."

"What did it say?"

"It said...it said none of us want to go home."

Then, like a rug is pulled out from under her feet, she drops to the ground, her knees pulled to her chest. She covers her face with her hands.

"And it's true," she says. "I don't. Or I do. But I don't."

"Neither do I," Henry says. When she says it out loud, it's like putting a key into a tiny door. When it swings open, light pours in. "I'm afraid if...if I go home..."

271

"That things will be exactly like they were," Ndidi says.

When she looks up, she and Henry lock eyes. Each sees the other flicker.

"Did you see that?" Henry whispers.

Ndidi nods.

They hold still, as still as deer. There is only silence on the mountain.

"We should hurry," Wolfson says. "We don't know when night can fall. Let's make torches and get moving."

Henry and Ndidi still stare at each other. When one nods, the other does too.

CHAPTER 27

Henry's mother says she was too young the first time they went camping to really remember, but she does. The way the air felt thick inside the tent. The way Henry could hear the rustling of night animals all around and above them. She remembers how the heat felt like a blanket until the chill set in like sudden ice. The higher she hikes with Ndidi and Wolfson, the more it feels like that night. She clutches the bear spray as they go, her whole body tense. This is what camping felt like, every time. She never understood how it made her father feel so free.

"Night's coming again," Wolfson says. He carries a small electric lantern that was in Henry's father's pack. She'd shown him how to use it. He doesn't think it will keep the beasts away, but the light is needed. It seems like the dark is even darker on the mountain.

And stranger. A mile back there was a rustle in the highest branches of the trees, and when the three of them looked up, a flock of birds flew backward out of the foliage. Like someone had recorded a video on their phone, then dragged their finger to the left, everything happening in reverse. Now beside them in the trees, just off the path, three bears sit watching them pass. Something about their eyes is raw—they feel human, like Wolfson's parents, but there's a hunger to them. She could never explain it, but things are exposed on the mountain. All her fears are swimming at the surface, and she can feel the bears seeing it and knowing. It makes her want to hide.

"Are you sure this is a good idea?" Ndidi says when the trees along the path begin to lean toward one another, their trunks weaving together like yarn.

"We're getting closer to the witch," Wolfson says without pausing. "It makes sense that things would get weird."

"Yes, okay. But I'm worried about how *much* weirder they'll get," she says quietly.

The path narrows, and Henry falls in behind them. It's as if the trees are squeezing them into single file. It's another thing Henry never liked about hiking—how the land is unpredictable.

"Watch out for that," Wolfson calls back, stepping over a

stick laid across the path. Ndidi steps over it, too, but when Henry reaches it, she bends down to pick it up. Perfect size for a walking stick. That was one part of hiking that she did like—finding the perfect stick. She was more interested in that kind of thing. Knowing what kind of tree it came from. Reading a book about all the things it could be used for. Books made her father restless. Rainy days, he'd read three pages, then go stand at the window, looking out. Always somewhere else to be. Something to find that he hadn't found yet.

"Henry, come on," Ndidi calls from around the bend. She sounds nervous, and when Henry turns the corner she sees why. There's a land bridge, an arc of rock that connects the part of the mountain they stand on to the next bluff.

Wolfson is already stepping out onto it, fearless, and Ndidi follows. Henry moves to follow them, walking stick in hand, but a moment later she stops in her tracks, staring after them.

They're both upside down, and they don't seem to notice. The land bridge has become a spiral, like the rock is clay that two invisible hands twisted into a loop.

"Wolfson! Ndidi!" Henry cries, and they turn back, startled. "You'll fall!"

Ndidi is closest, and the look on her face is puzzlement until it transforms into horror.

Then night drops.

As suddenly as a curtain released over a stage.

Something *slams* into Henry from behind.

She's being pulled backward, the hand not holding the walking stick clawing through grass and dirt. Ndidi screams. Rocks scrape Henry's stomach. A terrible snarling fills her ears, and there's an aching pressure around her foot. She kicks her other leg, twists her body as she's dragged backward.

It's one of the beasts.

Hulking white, its sparkling jaws are locked around her sneaker. With no moon in the black sky, the only light glows from the thing trying to kill her. She kicks her other foot wildly, then swings the walking stick she still grips in her left hand. She gets lucky—the end of the stick connects with one of the beast's eyes. It screams, momentarily letting go, and Henry tries to clamber to her feet. Off in the trees, she sees two more flashes of white dashing closer. More beasts. She's done for. Her foot throbs.

She swings the stick as hard as she can in a wide arc, trying to ward it away. The glowing jaws open and then close around the wood, splintering it. Its teeth are so close to her face, its breath in her eyes.

Ndidi appears, waving the torch they made at the campsite. The blaze of fire sends the beast scrambling backward, and off in the trees the other two moan like ghosts, freezing where they stand. Then Henry can breathe, the thickness of the beast's breath backing away and away, melting into the trees.

"You're right," Ndidi says, panting. Henry can barely understand her.

"What?"

"About the necklace," she says. "You left it in the hostel, didn't you? When Jamila was bitten."

"How did you...?"

"I noticed you weren't wearing it. When we were at the fountain. I wondered why. Then they said Jamila was in our room. And the beasts chased you o. To the Small Part. You're wearing it now, aren't you? They're chasing you. They're chasing *it*."

Henry's stomach drops.

"Do you think you're smarter than everyone? That we don't see?" Ndidi goes on when Henry doesn't answer. The dark has made a room around them. Trees that weren't there a moment ago now are, huddled close like they're listening. Far off, like an echo, Henry hears Wolfson calling for them.

"What are you talking about?" Henry pants.

"Something is wrong in This Place that's making it change," she cries. "And it's because of you. They're coming for *you*. Looking for *you*. Everything is strange because of *you*."

"That's not true," Henry protests. "The bats were already acting weird when I got lost. Wolfson said so."

"Yes, but the beasts didn't come until you did. Right? They only showed up when you arrived, Henry!"

She doesn't sound angry, only afraid and scrambling for answers. They stare at each other, and even with the beast gone Henry still can't catch her breath. Camping with her father, sometimes he would find a grasshopper, a moth, put it in a jar for her to look at. She feels like Ndidi has her in a jar.

"What am I going to do?" Henry whispers. "I don't know what to do."

But then Ndidi looks down and sees Henry's foot.

"Henry! You're bleeding o! Oh my gosh, Henry!"

She's right. Her shoe had been yanked partially off, and she sees the blood from the bite on her foot. Her stomach lurches.

"Oh no," she whispers. "Does that mean...?"

"Take off your shoe, quickly! Your sock too!"

With the sock and shoe off, they can see the bite more clearly. Not deep. A small puncture—the shoe and then beating the beast off with a stick saved her. But it doesn't matter. She can see the white just under her skin. The beast's poison.

"Henry...," Ndidi breathes, and she sounds more afraid than ever.

"It's okay," Henry says, trying to be brave. "We're already going to the witch. We just...we just have to get there. Right?"

Ndidi swallows and then nods. She watches Henry put her sock and shoe back on. Through the trees, Wolfson's calls are closer. Ndidi reaches out her hand to help Henry stand. Eye to eye, they grip hands for a moment longer.

"Up," Henry says.

Ndidi nods one more time.

"Keep going up."

CHAPTER 28

The beasts don't leave, and the suns don't rise. The night stays, and so do the beasts, trailing the three of them like phantoms. Henry swears she only ever saw two down in the town, but up here there are three. Then four. Then five. Henry and Wolfson and Ndidi make their way back through the woods, Henry carrying the torch and Wolfson carrying the lantern, looking over their shoulders so much they might as well be walking backward. When they reach the land bridge again, it doesn't look like a spiral anymore, but Henry warns them anyway.

"When you and Ndidi walked on it," she says, "it twisted. You know? Like you were upside down. You couldn't feel anything?"

"No," Wolfson says, frowning. He studies the land ahead, the rock stretching to the next bluff. "I felt a little dizzy? But I thought it was just the height. Should we ... ?"

"Is there another way to the top? Another path?" Ndidi asks.

Behind them, the white beasts inch closer. Henry waves the torch at them until they stop, crouching. Watching. They're no more than ten feet away. To go back would mean going through the line of them. There are six now.

"I don't think we have a choice but to go this way," Wolfson says, and the beasts' eyes seem to glimmer in agreement.

"What if we fall?" Henry researched hiking accidents in her father's absence. People think rock is so hard, but it can give way like brown sugar, crumbling into nothing.

"We won't," Wolfson says. He's already stepping out onto the land bridge. "If this is what we have to do, then we won't."

Henry thinks of what Christopher said: *This Place isn't as gentle as it used to be.*

"What if the witch has set it up like a booby trap?" Ndidi says, not following.

"I don't think she's that kind of witch."

Henry wants to argue. The beasts belong to the witch— nothing else makes sense. If she's not that kind of witch, then what kind is she?

Behind them, the beasts edge closer. Henry gives one more

wave of the torch, and then she and Ndidi follow Wolfson out into the dark, legs and hearts wobbly. The ground shimmers in the torchlight. Ahead, they can't see Wolfson's face but can hear him sniffle.

"Angie is okay, Wolfson," Ndidi says.

"I know."

Ndidi and Henry exchange a glance. Ndidi could have told him what she thought—about Henry and the necklace. How Henry wears a magnet around her neck, drawing the beasts from wherever their caves are buried. It would mean comfort, on one hand—wherever Henry is not, neither are the beasts. Which means they are not in the town. But wherever Henry is, the beasts are. Which means they are where Wolfson is.

But they plod on, Henry walking slower and slower until he and Ndidi get farther ahead. The distance lets her see the spiral. Ahead, Wolfson's walking upside down—or maybe he's right side up, and Henry is upside down?—and behind Henry are the white beasts. Her foot aches where she was bitten. She imagines the white spreading up.

"What *is* This Place?" she says, not for the first time.

"It's a dream, right?" Wolfson says over his shoulder. "It has to be a dream."

"And we're all here together?" Ndidi says.

"I guess so. Nothing else makes sense." He's silent for a minute, then adds: "It's been a very long dream."

"I don't sleep in dreams," Ndidi says.

"Maybe it's someone else's dream."

Henry feels dizzy the way Wolfson said she would. She doesn't feel like she's upside down, but when she looks ahead at the bluff they're walking toward, its peak points at the ground. By the time they reach the end of the spiral, her brain feels loose, like when she's been jumping on a trampoline for too long.

"We must be getting really close," Wolfson says. "Look."

They see animals, birds and squirrels and rabbits. All of them inside out. Their skeletons move like machines, their blood swimming around them like it's contained in an invisible sheath.

"What the...," Henry starts, but can't finish. Her heart beats so hard she can feel it thudding against her chest, as if it wants to escape. She's afraid to look down at her body and find that she's inside out too.

But Wolfson's and Ndidi's skin is still on the outside, and they stand staring at the blood rabbits, who hop about and nibble grass like everything is normal. For them it is. Henry wonders if her father saw these animals, if he'll remember when she gets home. Will she?

Behind them, the beasts growl, and Henry and the others start to walk again, quickly, leaving the spiraling land bridge behind. The path feels flat and steep at the same time—like

Henry's muscles are confused and so is the land. When it starts to sink under her feet, she's barely surprised.

"Henry, Ndidi...," Wolfson says, like he's warning them.

But it's too late.

The ground swallows them, grips them, and they go under. Henry can't breathe. She thinks of how she first fell into this world. She thinks of her father.

But not for long—the ground swallows them but then spits them out. Then swallows them again. She hears Wolfson and Ndidi gasping for breath and reaches out wildly, trying to grab them and hold on. She finds what she thinks is one of their ankles. The dirt and grit should feel rough, but instead it feels like silt, the silky texture of sand dug into underwater. The three of them come up again gasping, and Henry doesn't see the spiral bridge anymore. She tries to catch her breath, but the land swallows them once more, then heaves them onto grass a moment later.

"Ndidi," Wolfson gasps. "Henry?"

"Are you okay?" Henry tries to say. She's gagging on nothing. Unlike going underwater, nothing has made it into her mouth or lungs. None of this makes sense, and she wants to cry, but she hears her father's voice in her ear telling her that crying solves nothing. She hears it so clearly that she jerks her head, looking for his face.

No crying in camping, Henrietta, he says. *It attracts bears!*

"Dad?"

She sees him then, his back bright yellow with that pack he always carried. He hikes up a bluff that she didn't see before, the sky like an open window. She calls for him, but it's as if her words strike glass.

"Wolfson, that's my dad!"

But Wolfson is looking into the trees.

"There's a baby in there," he says, so low she almost can't hear. "It's crying. Can't you hear it?"

Henry does hear it. It wails louder and louder like a siren, and people shout, and one of them is Henry, calling for her father, but he won't look back. He just climbs and climbs, and the sky is so blue it makes her heart shrivel. Then she hears Ndidi crying, a silent cry. But Ndidi's face is smiling, tight and bright, like a cartoon. It's such a hard smile it makes Henry wince, and she also hears the beasts snarling and the baby crying and people shouting and Wolfson breathing like an engine, and all the colors of the world fall into one another like a pitcher poured over a watercolor painting.

Then suddenly it's silent, and the world looks different.

The mountain Henry's father was climbing is gone, and in its place is a small, neat house, white with a brick porch and a wide set of three steps. An old woman stands in the door. Her hair is as white and crisp as the paint on her home; her skin almost as brown-red as the bricks. She leans on a cane and looks at the three of them through small gold glasses.

"I'm sorry," she says. "This world was never made for children. Come on in."

CHAPTER 29

lowers hang in dried bunches from the witch's ceiling, and quilts are pinned to the wall. Food and food and food—four pots simmering on the stove. The oven glows with something baking, the smell of warm sugar filling the small house. It smells like memories, things Henry can almost remember but can't quite grab. Like a spot at the edge of her eye that disappears when she looks for it.

"Are you the witch?" Wolfson says. She told them to sit, but he stands near the door, looking lost. Henry can tell that the smell is stirring his brain, too, the memories somewhere inside like a paper boat drifting through rain.

"Come closer, and you will be less afraid," she says in answer. "Come sit by the water."

"The water...?"

None of them noticed the pool at first. It's in the center of the room, small and round like a koi pond. Wolfson, Ndidi, and Henry stand shoulder to shoulder, closer than they've ever been, huddled like sheep. They stare at the black water. No fish, but it seems full of lights—tiny and blinking, some of them traveling slowly like they're drifting through the ocean.

"Do you like lemonade?" the woman asks them, and all three nod. Her warm blue eyes focus in on Wolfson. "Do you remember lemonade?"

"I've had it here," he says quietly.

She laughs, a sound like wind chimes.

"No, you've had a version of lemonade. Here, let's see what you think of this."

She brings them cups made of thick bubbled glass and watches as they sip. For Henry, it tastes like lemonade—good lemonade. For Wolfson, something else is happening between his tongue and his brain. His eyes fill with tears. Henry freezes. She doesn't know how she didn't see it before—how he's been on the edge of crying since the second she met him.

"Ah, I thought so," says the witch.

A sound behind them turns them away from the sparkling black water.

The door to the witch's home, still open, is like a frame around what is coming up the stairs. The beasts, three of them, glittering white, teeth bared. Henry doesn't know how they'll fit through the door, but the look in their eyes—dilated silver—says they will try.

The first one leaps, and Ndidi screams, and Wolfson drops his glass, and the shards explode across the floor.

The beasts pass through the doorway—

And three black cats enter the house, one after another, on small, silent feet. Wolfson's eyes, still wet, are squeezed shut, and so he doesn't notice until one of the cats' plumy tails feathers his leg on its way over to the witch. Wolfson jerks, opens his eyes, gapes. The glass of lemonade that fell is somehow back in his hand, unshattered. The floor is clean. Ndidi sits with her hands clasped over her mouth.

"So they *are* yours," Henry breathes as the witch sinks into an armchair that wasn't there a moment before. She sips tea from a mug she hadn't been holding. "The beasts are yours?"

"Where did they...?" Wolfson says. "Are those the...?"

"They're mine," the witch says. "Now please tell me why you've come here."

Henry starts to speak, but Wolfson is quicker.

"A girl is hurt," he says. "And our donkey friend. In the village. One of your...cats? Bit her. People don't usually get hurt here. We don't know how to help."

"And Henry too," Ndidi says, pushing Henry closer.

"Henry?" Wolfson says, his eyes widening. "When?"

"Back there," she says. "I didn't want you to be scared. It barely hurts."

"Not just you," the witch says.

She beckons Wolfson closer, her eyes soft. He takes a hesitant step forward. She takes the sleeve of his shirt between two fingers, pushes it up a few inches. A glowing wound peeks out. White spiders up his arm.

"Both of you," the witch says softly.

"Wolfson," Henry gasps. "It bit you too?"

"At the balloon," he says, stuffing his sleeve down. "It's fine."

"Why didn't you tell us?" Ndidi cries. "At least with Henry we knew we were close! You walked all that way?" She turns to the witch. "Quickly, do you have bandages?"

"Little mother," the witch says softly. "Who cares for you if you do all the caring?"

Ndidi's mouth falls open. She steps away from Wolfson as if she's been struck.

"He needs help," Henry says. "So do Jamila and Eunice."

"And you thought you would find it here," the witch says.

"Yes," Wolfson says. "Angie told me about you a long time ago. How there was a woman at the top of the world. Eventually I realized that the person people called the witch was probably the same woman. I...I was going to come to you anyway." He glances at Henry and Ndidi, like he's wishing they weren't here. "About Angie. How to help her."

"I do prefer *Woman at the Top of the World* to *witch*," she says.

The Woman at the Top of the World takes the tea bag from her mug and blows a single puff of air on it from her lips. She places it on Wolfson's arm, and when she lifts it a moment later, the wound is gone. She motions for Henry to remove her shoe, and she repeats the gesture. Henry feels her pain melt away. It's like the wound was never there.

"Wounds of the flesh aren't the worst kind in This Place."

One of the black cats that used to be a sparkling beast has climbed onto her knees and laps tea out of the mug. The Woman at the Top of the World kisses her teeth and sets the mug on the floor, but then the cat sits next to it, staring up at her like a wolf stares at the moon. The other two do the same. Outside, three more white beasts come lumbering onto the porch. Henry and Ndidi watch as they pass through the doorway, becoming small black shadows that gather at the woman's feet. Six pairs of green eyes staring up at her. They stare and stare, and she stares back, until her eyebrows rise.

"Ah," she says, nodding to them in answer. Her eyes shift to Henry's face. "Yes, I think I do see the resemblance now. The eyes, and the ears. The same look in your eye, but a little more lost, even, than he was. It's been a long time, but here you are."

Then Henry's heart starts to burn, and when she falls to the floor, not even her friends can help her.

CHAPTER 30

t's not until the cats start batting at Henry's chest that she
realizes it's not her heart that's burning; it's her skin. The
skin right over her heart. When she hit the floor, the pain
shifted, scorching near her armpit. Then something soft, like
a feather.

A cat's paw. One of the Woman at the Top of the World's
shadows crouches near her shoulder, its soft paw inside her
shirt, batting as if at a moth. Henry looks down, panicking,
even though her father always told her not to panic, and she
begins to claw at her chest. Ndidi is at her side a second later,
and she's saying, "Your shirt is burning!" which doesn't make
sense, but she's right. A hole burning right through her shirt
in a perfect circle.

"It's...your necklace?" Wolfson says, confused. "It's your necklace! Take it off! Take it off!"

Henry pulls out some of her hair trying to rip the pendant off over her head. In her hands it still burns, but as she moves to throw it down, it twitches.

"What the...?"

It flies from her palms as if a giant magnet called it. It soars through the air and ends up in the open hands of the Woman at the Top of the World.

"What did you do to me?" Henry pants. She clutches her chest. She's afraid to look. She's still on the floor, where Wolfson and Ndidi grip her shoulders. The black cat has wandered casually back to the Woman at the Top of the World, who stares down at the pendant in her hands. When she does look up at Henry, her face is folded and sad.

"The answer is in the inverse, sweetie," she says. "As it so often is. Why are you here?"

"I—I'm here to help Wolfson to...," Henry starts, but the words are like water around a drain. The Woman at the Top of the World shakes her head, and Henry lets them slip away.

"Telling lies is not the way out of this place," the woman says. "Whether you tell them to yourself or others. Now, why are you here?"

"I...wanted to ask you a question."

"Ask."

"My father made a map," Henry says. "While he was here. He mapped all the places he saw. And he mapped this mountain. I just want to know if you met him. I want to know what he said."

"Why?"

To say it in front of Ndidi and Wolfson feels like pulling her heart out of her body, placing it on display like the objects in her father's basement.

"I just want to know why he was gone so long," she says softly.

The only sound is the purring of the cats.

"This won't be what you want to hear, my dear. But you'll have to ask your father."

Henry hangs her head. All this way, walking in his footsteps, and it led her only to more questions. The kind she couldn't bear to ask out loud.

"Let me see the map," the Woman at the Top of the World says.

Henry raises her head.

"My dad's?"

"There's only one map of This Place that I know of." She smiles and holds her hand out.

Henry draws it out of her pack, slowly passes it over. She watches the woman unfold it, a gentle smile on her lips.

"Ah, he didn't see as much as I thought he might've," she

says. "He's a slow learner, if you don't mind me saying so. Ah, but there it is. X marks the spot."

She turns the map around, pointing at the X Henry noticed at the top, in empty space.

"What is it?" Henry says.

"I'm surprised you haven't figured it out yet," she says. "You and your gathering of little pieces. I'll show you. Go to the window."

Wolfson and Henry look at each other, then at Ndidi. Outside, the night is as thick as oil. Henry finds it hard to believe they were out there, walking up the mountain, passing animals with skeletons outside their skins.

"Go," the woman says again, gently. "What do you see?"

Wolfson and Ndidi help Henry up, and they walk slowly to the window, eyeing the cats. They creep toward the glass and stare out.

Henry doesn't think any of them wants to be the one to say it, but eventually she does: "It's too dark. We can't see anything."

"And there is your answer," the woman says. "X marks an empty spot."

She holds up the necklace.

"Did my father steal that from you?" Henry asks, confused. A piece of beehive, yes, but a necklace?

"Not the necklace."

The pendant opens in her hands. There have never been hinges, so Henry doesn't know how she does it. But it twists open, and a silver light floods the room, so sudden and bright that even the cats blink and turn their faces.

"What is that?" Wolfson says from behind his hand, peeking through the cracks.

"It's what her father took."

The Woman at the Top of the World upends the pendant into her palm, and out pours the light, liquid and solid at the same time. It pools in the cup of her hand, and with the other hand she holds the empty pendant out to Henry, making her come close. She takes it—the metal is cold.

The light in the woman's palm pools and pools, gathering. It becomes round. It takes shape. It becomes solid. Eventually she's holding a stone, not altogether white but with swirls throughout it like shadow.

"An opal," she says. "This was my own father's gift to me. Long ago. Before This Place was made."

She extends her arm over the black pool at the center of her house and drops the opal down into its water. It doesn't even splash. It doesn't sink or float to the surface. It settles into the water like there's a bed for it Henry can't see.

Wolfson notices the light coming through the window first. He's still there at the windowsill with Ndidi, and when they turn to look back outside, Henry hears the breath catch in Ndidi's throat.

"The moon," Wolfson says, like he's just learned the word for the first time. "I haven't seen it for..."

Henry can feel him turning and seeing her, looking at her turned back. She's realized, too, staring down at the black sky in the Woman at the Top of the World's pool. Henry closes her eyes as a shield before he says what comes next:

"Your father stole the moon?"

CHAPTER 31

S ometimes we don't fully understand what has been done until we hear from who it was done to," the Woman at the Top of the World says quietly.

She tells the story in the silver light the moon casts through the window.

"I didn't know what to expect when your father climbed this mountain. Sometimes, since This Place was born, people will climb up because they assume the truth will be at the summit. But your father was different—an adventurer. He didn't seem too upset about being lost. He seemed disappointed when the door opened, when he found his way. He almost didn't go back. And maybe wouldn't have just yet, if they hadn't been chasing him."

She gestures down at the black cats, who all seem to nod their heads, purring.

"They couldn't follow, of course," she goes on. "I was surprised when my stone passed through. Some things go, some things don't. Everyone thinks I make all the rules. And it's true, I make some. But some things are beyond my control. It's been so many years—I'm glad to see the moon again."

"My dad only got back a few days ago," Henry says. "He was gone for a year."

"For you," she says, smiling sadly. "Time bends and twists and hugs itself when you're lost. When you go, that's one thing I would like you to remember. That your experience is yours. Not others'."

"How did you get to This Place?" Wolfson asks her. He's working very hard to not look at Henry. "Here?"

"I made it," the woman says. She lifts her arms. "When my home was taken from me, when my father was taken from me...I became lost. I exploded into grief. Then one by one the trees grew, and one by one the rabbits began to move. The ones closest to me, up here, aren't quite right. Too raw, I think. But down below, things are mostly all right, aren't they? Down there by the water? Little by little, things Became, all my memories trying to make a home here. Then birds came— not birds of my own creation. But real ones. And people. Everyone passing through. Something like a magnet in this place, drawing all of you near. I've gotten used to visitors—it's not their fault they're here, and it's not mine either. Lost is lost. Grief is grief. Never had someone steal from me, though," she adds.

Shame sweeps through Henry like the moonlight.

The Woman at the Top of the World presses her hand to her throat.

"You're ashamed?" she says. "Why are you ashamed?"

"How—how do you know what I feel?" Henry stammers.

"This is my home, this whole world. I see your feelings like the moon I see here in this water. I feel everything," she says. "You're walking inside my heart."

"I didn't know it was the moon," Henry says. She wants to cry, but she feels too empty to do it. "He gave me the necklace. I didn't know he stole anything."

She doesn't seem to notice Henry spoke. On the back of her armchair is a folded blanket, and she reaches up to stroke it.

"My love becomes blankets on your beds, knitted the way my grandmother taught me. My hunger becomes the food that grows in this strange land. I didn't know what my rage became until...well." She points at the cats, who go on purring. "Don't be ashamed of your shame. Shame means your compass isn't broken. It guides your steps."

Henry wants to look away, but she can't. She feels like a worm on a hook, squirming.

"It makes you uncomfortable to hear how I've been hurt," the Woman at the Top of the World says. "That's all right. But that doesn't mean I won't say it."

"I . . . I don't know what I'm supposed to do," Henry says to her. "About any of this. I came all this way to try to understand my father. To be like him. And now what?"

"Is that really why you're here?" she says gently. "Is it?" She pauses, then cocks her head at Henry. "Oh, you have one more question."

Henry's face burns.

"That's all right. You don't have to say this one out loud. But I'll answer: How can you be just like him? When you're a person who gives things back, who makes your own path?"

She turns away from Henry, toward Wolfson, toward Ndidi, who are still by the window, but squatted down now, petting the black cats.

"And you?" she says to Wolfson. "Are you going to stay? I feel you down there in the town, wondering and wondering. And now you're here. What are you going to do, young man?"

And there are Wolfson's tears again, the ones Henry didn't notice. The shame pulses through her again, harder.

"I don't know," he says. "I love my parents. But they're not my parents. They're wolves. And I love my home. But it's not my home. And I love Angie but she's . . . she's . . ."

"Your mother," the Woman at the Top of the World says,

and when his tears spill over, she nods encouragingly. "Angie is your mother now. It doesn't matter that she didn't give birth to you. Everyone is always trying to find their way out of This Place, but what if your way is to stay?"

She looks at Ndidi.

"It's time for you to go," she says. "You and Henry. But I have something I want to tell Wolfson before he goes back down the mountain. Wait on the porch. My rage will keep you company. They're much more friendly now that the moon has returned."

The porch is lit up silver in the moonlight. Ndidi and Henry stand side by side, staring up at it, the cats gathering around their feet.

"Where did she come from?" Ndidi says out loud. The cats answer.

They came to her town and burned all their homes, one of the cats says. *In Kentucky. In a place where people had started to gather things.*

Money and jewelry and heirlooms, gone, another says. *A whole town that was supposed to go on becoming. The whole top of their mountain soon after.*

Gone, says a third.

This is her home now. A home full of memories.

She lost her father that night. Some people wish on stars. Enola wishes on the moon. Having it back in the sky means everything to her. Everything.

Wolfson comes out of the small, neat house and stands beside them at the railing. The moon is starting to sink.

"A real night," he says.

"I wonder if the bats are happy," Ndidi says. "To see the moon again."

"I didn't know he took it," Henry tells them. "In my world he was gone for a year."

"I don't remember what a year is," Wolfson says. But his eyes don't look the way they've looked; his face isn't the face she's gotten to know in This Place.

"What did she tell you?" she asks him.

"My real name," he says.

"What is it?"

"Wolfson."

CHAPTER 32

They're far down the mountain when the suns rise. Even if Henry hadn't been to see the Woman at the Top of the World, she would know that something was different. It feels warmer, but she shivers at the same time. Behind them she can see birds perching on the spiral bridge—from here they look like they hang upside down.

"Why did your dad steal the moon?" Ndidi asks.

"I think he thinks he stole it for me. But I don't think that's true."

"Then why?"

"I think he's looking for something," she says simply.

They walk the rest of the way in silence, all the way down to the campsite that was her father's. The place where they lit the fire is still warm, but it feels like a hundred years since they were here.

"What was in the notebook?" Ndidi asks Henry, pointing. "The thing that made you cry."

It makes Henry want to cry again.

"It...it was something my dad wrote. All the way up here. He wrote, *Should I call Henrietta 'Henry'?* He always seemed so set on calling me Henrietta. Sometimes it seems like what he likes is the only thing that matters. But he wrote that."

"I don't think my mother knows my favorite color," Ndidi says. "My father either. Sometimes I think they only know how old I am because it makes me the oldest. But my favorite color is blue. And I want them to know that. To know lots of things about me."

"Are you going to tell them?" Henry asks. Then Henry's arms begin to flicker. Her hands in and out of sight.

"Henry—" Ndidi begins, but she stops abruptly, looking over Henry's shoulder. Henry looks to see what she sees, but it's only the tight embrace of trees. She hears Wolfson whisper her name. But then she hears something else.

Laughter. Distant, as if through floorboards. The sound of someone clapping. Then the smell of warm food, the snap of oil.

Ndidi's head tilts like a puppy's. She takes a step forward.

"I hear my cousin," she says. "I see my mother."

Her smile starts small, then grows, and grows.

"I see my mother," she says again. "And she's looking right at me."

She takes a step forward, and she's gone before her foot touches the soil, just as a door begins to crack in Henry's mind. When the door opens, there is forest on the other side.

"I thought you'd be gone by now," Wolfson tells her.

"Are you going to be okay?" Henry asks him. "Will you ever come back?"

"Yes," he says, smiling. "And no."

CHAPTER 33

Quinvandel smells of cedar and pine, and it calls her name.

With her back pressed to a tree, the dizziness passes like a hand over her eyes. It's night. Thick night, and the forest calls her name.

Not the forest.

Her mother.

Henry takes one wobbly step, and then another. Around her waist, her father's pack slides sideways. It's too dark to see, but she stuffs her hand inside. The paper of the map. The chain of the necklace.

More steps, the calling getting clearer.

Through the trees, white light. Not the light of beasts, but the bobbing glow of a flashlight.

Henry is on the path. She makes her way, slow and steady. The night is so dark, but she's not afraid. Down this hill is her house with the blue door. She can see the porch lights. She can hear her mother's voice. She can still hear the voice of the Woman at the Top of the World too: *How can you be just like him? When you're a person who gives things back, who makes your own path?*

"I'm coming!" Henry shouts up into the sky. "I'm here!"

She can hear her mother running. They're on a path back to each other. When they collide in the forest, her mother is sobbing, the flashlight fallen to the ground and illuminating their feet.

"Mom, how long?" Henry is saying over the sound of the tears. "How long was I gone?"

"Hours, Henry, hours! It's almost midnight; where have you been? We have to go see your father, he was so worried—"

Her mother talks, and Henry listens. She's saving her words for when the three of them are together. She can picture it now: the fluorescent light of the hospital, the little blinking stars of the tower that monitors her father's heart. It's not moonlight, but she'll pretend. She has an empty locket to give her father. She's on her own path.

She has many, many things to say.

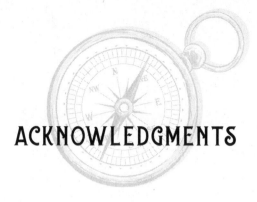

ACKNOWLEDGMENTS

I got lost in this book. My deepest thanks go to my editor, Alexandra Hightower, who found me in it. Alex, I firmly believe that you are the only person who could've done what you did for this book and helped me transform it into the shape I was desperately searching for. I'm eternally grateful. Thank you also to Crystal Castro—you are so sharp and so capable, and this book is better because of you.

Thank you to Patrice Caldwell and Trinica Sampson-Vera. I am so often like a one-person herd of cats, and your patience in shepherding me is so deeply appreciated. The New Leaf family's support of me and my work is something I don't take for granted.

This book exists in gratitude for the many people who have taught me what it means to grieve and what it means to explore—which is not, as we know, the same as what it means to discover.

May we all explore our grief. May we build worlds with it. May we come home, whatever home may be.

Aisha Asad

OLIVIA A. COLE

is a writer from Louisville, Kentucky. She teaches creative writing at the Kentucky Governor's School for the Arts, where she guides her students through poetry and fiction but also considerations of the world and who they are within it. She is the author of several books for children and adults, including her middle-grade debut, *Where the Lockwood Grows*. Olivia invites you to learn more about her and her work at oliviaacole.com and follow her on X @RantingOwl.